THAT BOY RED

THAT BOY RED

Rachna Gilmore

A NOVEL

Harper*Trophy*Canada™
An imprint of HarperCollins*Publishers*Ltd

Published by Harper*Trophy*Canada™,
an imprint of HarperCollins Publishers Ltd

First edition

Harper*Trophy*Canada™ is a trademark of HarperCollins Publishers Ltd.

HarperCollins books may be purchased for educational, business,
or sales promotional use through our Special Markets Department.

HarperCollins Publishers Ltd.
2 Bloor Street East, 20th Floor
Toronto, Ontario, Canada
M4W 1A8

www.harpercollins.ca

Library and Archives Canada Cataloguing in Publication information is available

ISBN 978-1-55468-459-5

Printed in the United States
RRD 9 8 7 6 5 4 3 2 1

In memory of John Gilmore, whose stories started it all,
and
in memory of Martin Gilmore, whose stories moved it forward,
and
for the extended Gilmore family, who filled in the gaps.

CONTENTS

THAT BOY RED

CAT-LESS GRANNY

RED HAD JUST MANAGED TO GET THAT TIRE rolling at a fair clip between the barns when the train whistle shrilled through the air. He stopped dead in his tracks, and the tire flopped to the ground in a cloud of red dust.

"Jumpin' Jerusalem!" Red took off on the run.

Not across the turnip field and through the hollow to the station to see the train, all sooty and tired from pulling two passenger cars, and maybe eight freight cars, the steam billowing impatiently from its stack—but straight to the wellhouse.

Ellen would have a conniption if he didn't . . .

Red worked the pump vigorously, up and down, up and down, filling the bucket with gushes of water. He ran with it to the back door, spilling a good bit on the way.

1

The train whistle shrilled again, long and gloating—
Hooo! Fooool! Hooo! Fooool!

Red charged into the back porch.

It was hot as blazes in there. Red's older sister, Ellen, had the fire roaring in the stove—it was always moved to the far end of the porch for the summer to save the house from the heat. Ma and Ellen had spent hours cooking a special dinner, for all it was a weekday and plenty of work still waiting.

Red dumped some water from the bucket into the basin and dipped up hot water from the tank attached to the stove.

Ellen looked up, her face flushed with heat as she mashed potatoes at the table. "For goodness' sake, Red! I told you ages ago—"

"All right, all right, I'm gettin' cleaned up," said Red, trying to work up a lather with the homemade lye soap.

"You should *be* cleaned up by now," said Ellen. "Did you put the cats in the barn?"

"Yes, and they were none too happy about it." Red scrubbed his hands.

"What about Ma's trick gadgets? Did you—?"

"I'm just about to, if you'd give a fella a chance—"

"For mercy's sake! Pa and Ma will be back any blessed minute with—"

"I'm hurryin' fast as I can." Red sloshed his hands in

2

the basin. "Why didn't you get Mac to do it?"

"Mac was studying, unlike you," said Ellen, opening the oven door to check the roast. "And he's waiting outside for the buggy."

Red tried to slick back his thatch of unruly brown hair. "There! That do?"

"Tuck in your shirt, you clown. You weren't born on a raft!" Ellen clanged shut the oven door. "Now get those gadgets out of sight, and make sure Bunch set the table straight." Her eyes twitched to the clock on the wall as she wiped her forehead.

"Who d'you think you're bossing?" muttered Red. Seemed like ever since Ellen had got the licence to teach at his school, she'd taken on the licence to nag him even more at home.

Not that he really blamed her this time for being in such a kerfuffle.

They were all in a kerfuffle.

It was like that every year when Cat-less Granny came to stay with them.

Red hurried into the kitchen where they always ate, even when the stove was moved into the back porch. The big table Pa had built was by the side window, overlooking Ma's vegetable garden, which was filled with lines of upright onions, red-leafed beets, bushy beans, lettuces and tomato plants. On the other side of the white slat fence was the turnip field, the straight drills of deep-green turnips alternating with strips of red soil.

The table, set with Ma's best silver and china, was all sparkling and polite. As far as Red could see, everything was good and straight enough.

He reached over to the windowsill and snatched up the spoon with the fly, and the package of gum that snapped at your fingers. Ma had taken them out yesterday when Stew Gillis had dropped by with his cousin. Everyone in Applecross already knew about that spoon—it was from Ma's old days working for the Eaton's catalogue over in Manitoba, before she'd married Pa—but Stew's cousin had never seen it. How they'd laughed when he'd tried to shake that fly off, all furtive and embarrassed. It was a shame, though, to put that gum away; Ma had only just bought it, and they'd barely had the chance to use it.

Red sighed. They wouldn't be seeing either of those gadgets for a long while.

He whipped over to the sitting area at the other end of the room. On the windowsill behind the sofa, Ma's geraniums flowered all bright and cheerful, as though unmindful of the impending doom. He opened the side cupboard and shoved the spoon and gum to the very back, next to Ma's whoopee cushion.

For a glorious moment Red imagined putting that cushion under Cat-less Granny's chair. He snorted with nervous laughter. Granny would skin him alive, if Ma or Ellen didn't do it first.

Bunch, who was seven, came trotting from the parlour with Ma's green cut-glass dish for the bread-and-butter pickles. She handed it to Ellen and ran back into the sitting room.

"Do I look all right, Red?" she asked, swirling her good blue dress.

"You look just dandy, Bunch." Red squeezed her shoulder.

Poor Bunch. Her braided hair was so tightly pulled back it made zigzags along her forehead. Her bare feet were spotless, except for the mosquito bites, and her small hands were blotchy from scrubbing.

Red glanced furtively at his own hands and picked at the dark line under his thumbnail.

Cat-less Granny couldn't abide *durrt*.

Durrt, along with disorder, idle hands, noisy children, impudence, jokes and cats. Clover and Tubbs had mewed something pitiful when he'd shut them up in the barn. The cats were used to having the run of the house, during the day, at least.

Red swung his arms nervously and looked out the sitting room window.

On the other side of the front lawn was a scattering of apple, cherry and plum trees. Beyond them, the wheat field, with blue-green, knee-high grain, sloped down to the Sprucecliffe Road. Nicholson's field on the other side of the road was bushy with dark-green potato plants, now studded with creamy blossoms, showy as a parade.

Mac, who was two years older than Red, stood outside by the verandah, waiting for the buggy. His hands were in his pockets and his face was untroubled.

It was all right for him, thought Red sourly. Mac was Granny's favourite.

Red squinted against the evening sun to the right of the house, where the turnip field dipped down into the scrubby hollow filled with wild blueberry vines. Above the tangle of spruces on the other side, he could just make out the steam fuming from the train as it began to chug to the next station.

Red's breath escaped in a ragged sigh as he saw Flash and the buggy coming down the road. Of course, Ma and Pa had to take the horse and buggy for Cat-less Granny, never mind it was barely a ten-minute walk to the station.

"Ellen," called Red, as Flash trotted up their lane.

Ellen whipped off her apron and hurried to the sitting room, smoothing her navy-blue dress. Bunch crept up beside Red and stuck her damp hand into his.

Outside, Mac went over to hold Flash.

Red turned away as he caught sight of Granny's cushiony pink face and fluffy grey hair.

"Here she comes again, to boss us around and run this place," he said.

"You'd better behave, Red, I'm warnin' you!" Ellen twisted his ear, then twitched his shirt straight. "And wipe that look off your face."

Red scowled harder. "It not your hair she's always—"

"Shh!" Ellen dug her fingers into his shoulder.

Cat-less Granny stepped into the kitchen—along with a swirl of air that felt spitefully chilly for July. She wore a beige dress, patterned with stingy brown flowers, and a faded wool knit cardigan. Her sharp blue eyes seemed to take in everything. It was funny how she sucked up so much space, even though she was tiny and Ma towered over her.

"Ellen," said Granny. "You're looking fine. Best get married while you're still in your prime. Your young man won't wait forever. Enough of your teaching nonsense."

Ellen's colour rose, but she said nothing. She and Stewart Gillis had been going together for a while. They were always fighting and making up, but Red knew that Ellen wasn't about to get married 'til she'd paid their brother Alex's way through college.

Red saw Ma's lips tighten, as though to bite back a retort.

"Roderick." Granny's eyes pierced through Red. "Hmmph. Growing, I see." Her tone said plain as plain *bad weeds grow fast*. She sniffed as she glanced at his hair.

"Hello, Granny," said Red. He jerked up the corners of his mouth, as Ellen poked him in the back.

Cat-less Granny's eyes may or may not have softened as they turned to Bunch.

"Lucy. My. You're getting to be a big *gurrl*. A good *gurrl*, I hope."

Bunch ducked behind Ellen. Red wished he were small enough to join her.

"And where's Alex?" asked Cat-less Granny, looking around.

"Oh, he's in Charlottetown this summer," said Pa. "Workin' to save extra money for college."

Granny sniffed.

Ma said, "He was sorry he couldn't be here to greet you, Ma, but he couldn't pass up that job. Not when paid work's so hard to come by."

Cat-less Granny sniffed again.

Red wished that he too could be thirty miles away in Charlottetown.

He glanced at the clock. Cat-less Granny had been there barely five minutes and already it felt like an eternity. How long would she stay this time before moving on to the next of her six children? Granny rotated among them at her will—except for Aunt Bessie and her husband. To hear Cat-less Granny tell it, Aunt Bessie had said unforgivable things; but from what Red had overheard Aunt Bessie say, it sounded more like Granny had started it, and Aunt Bessie had decided not to take it any more. Red wished Ma could be less polite, so Granny'd stay away from them, too.

They sat down to a supper as elaborate and lavish as any Sunday dinner, instead of the usual weekday leftovers. But Red couldn't dig into the roast pork and gravy with his normal gusto. Everyone was subdued and polite—Ma rigidly pleasant, with none of her spark or laughter, and even Pa quieter than usual. The air almost felt squashed. It wasn't exactly like being at a funeral, thought Red. More like when the hearse went by, and you took off your cap and lowered your head, all solemn and sorrowful.

Cat-less Granny described her journey from Uncle Graham's place into Boston, where she'd caught the train, and the terrible long lines she'd seen for the soup kitchen: those poor jobless folks, some of them lookin' so wild and fierce, *och*, she was glad she didn't live in Boston, she'd never sleep a wink for worrying about being robbed, although dear knows there was little enough to rob, and strange folks aplenty coming to the countryside, and wasn't it a mercy Graham's job was steady and not lost in the Depression. Then she started in about Uncle Graham and Auntie Beryl's three girls, and how they were so well behaved, neat and polite, you'd think they were practically angels—except Red knew, from when they'd come up last summer, that they were more like little devils. Why didn't Granny stay longer with them if she thought they were so perfect?

Red scraped up the last of his lemon meringue pie and sucked his fork clean. He'd have asked for seconds except he knew Cat-less Granny would skewer him with a greedy-pig look, even if she didn't come right out and say so.

But when Mac finished his pie, Granny smiled at him and said, "Did you get enough to eat, dear?"

Mac nodded with a good-boy smirk that made Red want to punch the living daylights out of him. Wait 'til the next time they played war in the little barn. He'd run out from behind the binder—the slanted side of the big machine they used for cutting and binding grain into bundles was their battleship—and he'd tackle old Mac. He'd smush his face into the barn floor, even if Mac went rat-a-tatting at him, expecting him to fall down dead.

● ● ●

It was a relief that evening to get out of the house into the clean air and help Pa milk the cows, feed the pigs and water the livestock. Mac whistled tunelessly as they carried buckets of water from the pump to the wooden trough in the pasture. Mac's whistling had never both-ered Red before, but today it irked. It irked like a thorn in the foot. What right did Mac have to be so unconcerned?

At bedtime, when Red went upstairs to the big loft he shared with his brothers, he bumped into Mac. As he changed into his pyjamas, he trod on Mac's foot.

"Watch it, you!" Mac pushed him away.

"Watch it, yourself!" Red shoved back.

Then they were at it.

"Boys! What in the world d'you think you're doing?" Pa stood at the top of the stairs. "Your Granny just arrived, and here are you two making a rumpus!"

Red and Mac hung their heads. "Sorry, Pa."

They got into their own beds silently, their backs to each other.

After a while, Mac whispered, "Red."

Red ignored him.

"Red. Did you ever notice how Granny snorts, when she says *och*?" Mac snorted.

Red choked down his laughter. He was not about to give Mac the satisfaction.

"You *durrty, durrrty* wee boy!" whispered Mac.

Laughter spurted out of Red's nose and he turned around to grin at Mac.

Maybe it wasn't all Mac's fault that he was Granny's favourite. Now that Red thought about it, Mac had been the one to come up with the name Cat-less Granny, to distinguish this Granny from their other one, Pa's Ma, who'd died years ago. Red couldn't remember much about her except that she'd loved cats—and all her grandchildren.

• • •

That first week was the worst for Red.

It always was, when Cat-less Granny came.

He must never run in the house, or let the cats in, or slam the screen door. He must mind his p's and q's and never speak out of turn, because children should be seen and not heard. He must say, "Yes, Granny," instead of "Sure," and scrub his nails just about raw, and everlastingly wash his hands and face—more than the good Lord ever intended.

But worse than all of that put together was the display of Cat-less Granny's switch when they had visitors.

Each time, Granny would send him, Mac or Ellen to fetch that white linen bundle. It was kept in the parlour, in the good walnut bureau, along with Ma's best dishes. *Are you surrre yer hands are clean, Roderick? Can't have a durrty lad handling that.*

Red would have to carry the white bundle over to Cat-less Granny on his outstretched hands, palms up.

Granny would say to the visitors, "Well, since you asked to see it . . ."

That always boiled Red's britches, because hardly anyone ever *asked* to see it.

"Yes, dear," Granny would say. "You wouldn't think to look at it now, but my hair used to be red as red." She pronounced it *raid as raid.* "And it stayed that colour until it turned grey. Not like Roderick's, here." Her steely eyes bored into Red. "I can't think why they call you *Raid* still. Your hair hasn't been *raid* since you were a wee babe. It's no more than a *durrrty bruhn.*" Granny's tone always implied that Red must have done it on purpose, just to insult her.

Then Cat-less Granny would unroll the white linen cloth and triumphantly hold up the two-foot switch of red hair, tied at the top with black ribbon. Everyone would admire it, and Red's face would ache, trying to smile politely—lips closed, teeth gritted.

• • •

On the second Sunday after Granny arrived, they'd just finished dinner when Red heard the sound of a car in the distance. Still in his good Sunday clothes, he ran out into the sunshine and took off down the lane. Dr. MacLeod and Alex Stewart, the section lineman, were the only ones with money enough for cars, so it had to be one of them, if it wasn't a complete stranger.

Red whooped when he saw Dr. MacLeod's shiny black car slowing to turn in to their lane. The doctor and his wife were coming for a visit.

He sprinted towards the car, shouting hello. As the car passed him, he raced back after it, unmindful of the dust. No matter how fast he ran, he still couldn't catch the car. It could do over fifty miles per hour when it got going— way faster than Flash, even when he took the notion to run away.

The car stopped at the top of the lane, at the side of the house. Dr. MacLeod, short and round, with bushy grey eyebrows, climbed out and called hello. Mrs. MacLeod waved, the feathers in her hat nodding with each step up to the verandah and front door.

Red ran up to the car and walked around it, gently touching the sides and mirrors. The sun winked and gleamed in the chrome. It was something else, that car. Dr. MacLeod had given him several rides. When Red and Mac played car in the little barn—with the binder being the car—Red never wanted to be the passenger. He always wanted to be the driver and toot the horn, all busy and important.

Everyone was in the parlour when Red went inside. The MacLeods asked about Granny's trip and the family in Boston. Granny told them about the new car Uncle Graham had bought from some highfalutin fella who'd had to sell it cheap because he'd lost everything in the stock market crash, and thank goodness her children never had the money to put in that stock market, whatever it was. Cat-less Granny soured her mouth like she'd sucked on a lemon, and nodded.

There was a sagging silence.

Then Mrs. MacLeod, who was a good friend of Ma's and knew Granny's routine, asked, "Now, do you still have that switch of hair from when you were young? It would be a right treat to see it again. Such lovely hair." Her eyes twinkled apologetically at Red, then at Ma, who briefly touched Red's back.

Cat-less Granny smiled and favoured Ellen with the task of bringing out the white linen bundle. After everyone had finished admiring the hair, Granny laid it carefully on top of the cloth on the side table, beside Ma's precious copy of *Birds of North America*.

When The MacLeods got up to leave, they invited Granny for a ride to try out their car. Ma wanted to borrow a new quilting pattern from Mrs. MacLeod, so she went also, along with Bunch and Pa. Ellen headed outside to the verandah, to say goodbye.

"Malcolm, Roderick." Granny turned before leaving the parlour. "Stay here and put my hair away. Nice and *carrrefully,* mind." It was still on the side table, on top of the cloth, where she'd left it on display.

"Yes, Granny," said Red and Mac.

They watched from the front parlour window as the car turned around and purred down the lane. Red heard Ellen come back inside and start to rattle things in the kitchen, but he stayed glued to the window 'til the car disappeared.

Pa said he didn't see much point putting money into a car. He said he'd rather his children got their education so they could buy their own cars later on in life. Pa had borrowed money to put Ellen through Prince of Wales College, so she could get her teacher's certificate, and she was to put Alex through, and he'd put Mac through, and so on down the line. Red knew it made sense, but part of him still wished they could have a car. Flash was so . . . horsey. So smelly and unpredictable. A car didn't run away on you like a horse, or drop stuff from its rear end.

"Come on," said Mac. "Let's put away Granny's hair."

Reluctantly, Red turned away from the window.

He eyed the switch.

There it lay, all smug and boastful on the white linen cloth.

What was so wonderful about it, anyway?

As Mac began to lift the edge of the white cloth, Red

suddenly leaned forward and picked up the switch.

"What're you doing?" said Mac. "Put it back."

Red held out the switch at arm's length, and gave it a flick.

"Stop foolin' around, Red. Put that down."

"*Stop foolin' around Red, put that down,*" mimicked Red. He snapped the switch back and forth.

"Red, put it back. Right now."

"*Put it back. Right now,*" said Red.

"Red, I'm tellin' ya—"

"Silence!" Red cracked the switch. "I'm Cat-less Granny," he said in his best Scottish accent. "And I have her wicked witch switch. You will obey when I crack it."

"Now, hold on just a—"

"Be silent!" Red snapped the switch again. "The switch commands it. Stand yerself to attention."

Mac grinned uncertainly, then stood to attention.

A burst of power surged through Red. "By the Power of the Switch, I compel thee to stand on one foot."

Mac hesitated, then stood on one foot.

"Hop around the parlour three times."

"Three times!" cried Mac. "That's—"

"The Power of the Switch compels thee." Red cracked the switch again, the glorious, powerful switch.

Mac, choking with laughter, began to hop around the parlour. He crashed into the corner of the pump organ.

"Boys," called Ellen. "You know you're not to play in there. Go on outside."

Red turned an alarmed face to Mac, then, grinning, dashed to the side window behind the sofa. He pushed it up and climbed out, still gripping the switch.

"Red, you can't—" began Mac.

"The Power of the Switch compels thee!" said Red. "You must follow and obey."

Mac flung himself out of the window. "Give it to me. It's my turn. Give it now!"

"Come and get it!" Red sped towards the barns, snapping and waving the switch.

"Give it," shouted Mac. "Or I'll pound you."

Red sprinted down the worn track between the little barn and the big barn, past the henhouse and over the gate into the pasture field. He whooped and hollered, whipping his powerful red switch. The cows lying in the shade of the hedgerow, chewing cud, stared with superior, bland eyes.

Mac came thudding behind Red.

Red swung around. "By the Power of the Switch I compel thee to stop."

Mac stopped—and toppled over onto a dry cow patty.

He sprang to his feet, dusting his pants.

Red turned and ran, with Mac giving chase.

"Give it," shouted Mac. "Or I'll make you pay."

Red raced across the field. He was laughing so hard, he began to get a stitch in his side. Jean, their large, mild workhorse, turned her head to look at him, then went back to chomping on a clump of clover.

Mac almost caught up, but Red swerved just in time and Mac tumbled to the ground again.

Bent over double, Red gasped with laughter.

Mac lunged at his legs and they both went sprawling. As they tussled on the grass, Mac tried to grab the switch, but Red rolled aside, still gripping it.

Then something squished against Red's hand, and he dropped the switch. The hot stink of raw cow dung exploded up his nostrils. "Ugh."

Red wiped his hand again and again through a patch of clean grass, then leapt to his feet.

He froze.

Mac stood motionless, with the switch in his hand.

The long red hair was tangled and snarled. And slimy with green dung.

The glory and power of the game vanished faster than a punch.

"What're we going to do?" Mac's eyes were stricken.

"I dunno." Red's mouth went dry. "I'm not the oldest. You're the oldest."

"You're the one started it—"

"If you hadn't chased me, if you'd waited your turn—"

"Shut up!" snapped Mac.

Red flinched. Pa never let anyone say that, and Mac wasn't usually the forceful type. It had to be pretty dire, for Mac to say that.

Red wiped his shaking hands against his pants. "We . . . we can wash it, can't we? In the stream? Back of the other pasture?" It was on the other side of the little barn, next to the mixed field of pale-green barley and oats.

"Look at it." Mac shook the dung-covered switch. "Does it look like it'll wash in a stream? We need soap, at the very least."

Red licked his lips. "Okay. So we'll . . . I'll go get it. From the back kitchen."

"Yeah?" said Mac in his know-it-all voice. "And how long d'you think it'll take to dry the hair? Or were you planning to put it back soakin' wet?"

Red felt the blood drain from his face as he remembered something else. "Mac, we didn't put away the cloth. It's still on the table . . ." He trailed off, at a complete loss for words.

Mac began to blink hard, the way he did when he was thinking.

Red looked hopefully at him.

From the stable end of the barn, Red heard Flash snorting, as though he wanted out. Pa had put him in there after church in case they needed him to go visiting.

At last, Mac cleared his throat. "Maybe . . ."

"What?"

"Maybe . . . we can scrape it clean," said Mac. "Against a tree. You know, take the worst of it off?"

"Scrape." Red nodded. "That's it. And the rest will just dust off. Won't it?"

Somewhere inside him he didn't think it would work, but he couldn't bear to think of that. They had to do something, anything, before Cat-less Granny got home . . .

They raced to the line of spruce, poplar and other assorted trees dotted along the wooden rail fence between the pasture and the potato field. Mac headed for the big willow—it had the roughest bark. He hesitated, then held out the switch to Red.

Red took it.

He figured he had to. It was only fair.

Drawing in a deep breath, he scraped the filthy switch against the trunk.

Bits of hair snapped off and clung to the bark.

In a panic, Red swiped it again and again, hoping the hair would somehow scrape off the trunk and back into his hand.

"Stop it, you idiot," yelled Mac.

Red stopped, too scared to resent the *idiot*.

Strands of dung-streaked hair fluttered mockingly from the tree; in his own fist were just a few wisps of hair, and the black ribbon that had once held it together.

A fly buzzed around the tree and settled on the hair. Red heard Flash snort again, from the stable.

"What do we do, Mac?" Red's voice cracked. He couldn't help it.

Mac shook his head, as though in a daze. "Dunno. But we've got to find some hair. Red hair. Put it in the cloth."

"Find hair." Red nodded. "That's it. Red hair."

He heard an indignant whinny from the stable.

"Where the deuce are we going to find red hair?" said Mac.

Red's mind whirled like a dust storm. In the distance, Flash continued to snort and carry on. He sure had a temper. It kind of went with his . . .

Red snapped around to stare at the whitewashed barn across the field.

"That's it," he cried.

"What?"

"Flash!"

"What d'you mean, Flash?"

"Flash's tail. It's red. Let's cut some off, and—"

"Are you completely daft?" said Mac. "D'you think no one'll notice the difference between horse hair and real hair? D'you think *she* won't notice?"

"It'll buy time," said Red. "'Til we find some real hair. Least for now it'll look like there's something in that cloth—"

"That's the stupidest, most foolish—"

"Have *you* got a better idea?"

Mac's mouth opened. Then shut.

Red figured that pretty much covered it.

"All right," said Mac, blinking hard. "We'll need scissors."

"I'll get 'em from the kitchen."

"No, you can't let Ellen see you like that."

Red looked down at his Sunday shirt, pants and good shoes. They were streaked with dung. Ma would have a fit, but that was the least of his problems.

He creased his forehead and thought hard, harder than he ever did, even for spelling bees.

"Pa's good workshop scissors," he said. "I left them by the sleigh in the little barn."

For once Red was glad he'd forgotten to put them back, even though Pa was always complaining, "Now, where did that boy go leave my tools?"

Mac nodded eagerly. Red released the last strands of hair from his hand and crammed the black ribbon into his pocket. They raced across the field, Mac going to the stable, Red to the little barn. Red hunted for the scissors in the back corner where he'd been cutting sandpaper to smooth the wooden puppet he'd carved for Bunch. Clover, a grey cat with white patches, came running over to rub against his legs. Red gave her a quick pat, found the scissors and ran over to the stable end of the big barn, where Mac was waiting.

Together, they crept towards Flash's stall.

Flash whinnied and rolled a warning eye at them.

Red gulped. "You hold him, Mac. You're the one likes horses." Horses were such chancy critters.

Mac opened his mouth to argue, then shrugged.

"Best lead him out of the stall," said Red. "I don't want my head kicked in."

Tubbs, their fat calico cat, who was perched on an exposed beam on the inside of the barn, watched them with unblinking golden eyes.

Mac sidled up to Flash. "Here, boy. Nice and slow, now. Easy, easy." He patted Flash's muzzle. Gently, he took down the bridle from the wall, and put it on Flash.

Flash neighed, almost like he knew what was coming. Tubbs shot off like he *did* know what was coming and wanted no part in it.

Red took a few steps back. That was the *darn* trouble with horses—he allowed himself the comfort of that forbidden word—they had too much a mind of their own. Especially old Flash.

Slowly, talking soothingly, Mac led Flash out from his stall.

"Quick," he said. "I can't hold him forever."

Red edged over to Flash's rear end. The tail wasn't really that red, but . . .

Flash backed up, snorting.

"Hold him, will you!" said Red.

"I'm trying. Get on with it. Now."

Red grabbed a hunk of Flash's tail, and cut it with the scissors.

Flash neighed and kicked up his hind legs.

Red crashed to the barn floor along with Mac.

By the time Red got to his feet, Flash was gone, doing what he did best—running away.

"Why didn't you shut the door?" said Mac, sitting up.

"Why didn't you hold him?"

"I did. If you hadn't scared him, he'd never have run."

"I had to get this, didn't I?" Red held up the chunk of coarse, reddish-brown hair.

They both stared at it.

It didn't look much like Cat-less Granny's hair.

Red cleared his throat. "It looks like Granny's hair. Doesn't it?"

"Sure it does." Mac nodded. Too hard. "But we've got to get Flash back, before Pa—"

"We've got to put this hair away first," said Red.

"We need something to tie it with."

Shoving the scissors into his pocket, Red pulled out

the ribbon. He gripped the hair with both hands while Mac fumblingly tied the ribbon around it.

Together they sprinted across the yard, past the well-house to the side porch.

Heart thundering, Red peered into the window.

Ellen.

He turned a panicked face towards Mac.

Mac motioned with his hand. With a surge of relief, Red understood. Of course. They'd get back into the parlour the way they'd got out. Mac was the smartest brother; no wonder he was the best speller in school.

Red and Mac crept around along the side of the house to the parlour window and climbed in. The parlour, basking in the late-afternoon sunshine, looked peaceful and polite, as if it had never heard the word *dung*. Dust motes floated about like they hadn't a care in the world.

Red tiptoed over to the table. Reverently, he laid down Flash's tail on the white linen cloth and reached for its edge.

"Wipe your hands," whispered Mac fiercely.

Red looked at his hands, rubbed them against his pants, then reached for the cloth again.

"What in the world?"

Red and Mac jerked around.

Ellen stood in the doorway with the green cut-glass dish in her hand.

Her eyes fell on the white cloth and her jaw dropped. "Where's Granny's hair?"

Red and Mac looked at each other.

Red found his voice. "It's like this," he said. "We were playing. It was the Power of the Magic Switch, and . . ." He blundered on, with Mac chipping in the odd word.

Ellen's eyes grew rounder and rounder. Her hand went up to her mouth. Then she collapsed onto a chair, laughing.

"It's not funny," said Red.

Ellen looked up. She tried to speak, but she couldn't. She just pointed at the horse hair, then at them, and shrieked with laughter.

Red looked again at the hair. It was *nothing* like Cat-less Granny's. It lay, bold and horsey—like a vulgar oath—on that innocent white cloth.

He began to laugh too, along with Mac.

Ellen wiped her streaming eyes and gasped, "It's no' even the same colour, but a *durrty bruhn*!"

That set them all off again. Red's stomach ached, but he couldn't stop laughing.

Then a shriek tore through the air.

Red swung around. His laughter died as if it had been chopped with an axe.

Cat-less Granny stood at the door, along with Ma, Pa and Bunch.

Ma looked shocked and Bunch's mouth was open. Pa's eyes swerved from the mess on the table to the boys.

"What is that thing?" cried Granny. "*Wheeer* is my *heeair? Wheeer* is my *heeair?*"

"Red. Mac. What have you been up to?" asked Ma.

Red tried to find his voice. It seemed to be drowned in a bottomless well.

"Boys," said Pa. "What's the meaning of this?"

Mac broke the silence. "We were just playing," he began.

Red couldn't let Mac take the blame. "It was me," he managed to croak. "Just a game. It was the Power of the Switch, see, and—"

"The what?" said Ma.

Cat-less Granny, quivering with fury, glared at them.

"The Power of the Switch. A magic wand, like. It gave you power, whoever had it. And we didn't think and we went out, and . . ."

Ma shook her head, like she was dazed. Her hand went up to her mouth.

"The Power of the Switch?" Pa's shoulders seemed to be shaking.

"That thing?" said Ma, in a strangled voice. "Is it from Flash? Is that why we saw him running away?" Her face was solemn, but a glimmer at the back of her blue eyes gave Red some hope.

Shamefacedly, Red nodded.

"You wicked, wicked lads," gasped Cat-less Granny. She turned to Ma. "Is this how you raise your boys, Kathleen? Like hoodlums? Hooligans? I gave you my hair to keep, to cherish and remember me by."

"Ma, I'm sure the boys didn't mean—"

"Duncan, I hope you'll teach your lads a lesson," continued Granny, as though Ma hadn't even spoken. "With a real switch. I recommend you cut a long, stout stick from the woods and *whale* some manners into them."

Red's knees turned weak. Pa never hit them; he never lifted his hand to them.

"Go and find Flash, boys," said Pa. "And Red, put away my scissors. Then both of you, come and see me in the barn."

"But first, change out of your Sunday clothes," said Ma. "The dirt of them . . . I never saw the like."

"Whip them hard," cried Granny. "Whip them good. That was a precious family heirloom, and now it's gone."

Red changed out of his good clothes, then put the scissors back in the workshop at the near end of the little barn. Together, he and Mac went to find Flash.

It took a while.

They finally spotted Flash in a neighbour's distant

pasture field; he was chewing on a clump of clover, and didn't seem to be of any mind to go along with them.

By the time they'd chased Flash several times around the field, got him down to Sprucecliffe Road and up their own lane, it was near suppertime. They led Flash into the pasture, shut the gate tightly, then went to see Pa, who was waiting for them in the big barn. Heads down, they stood in front of him.

Pa's face was sober, his broad forehead lined, as though with weariness and disappointment. "Boys, what you did was thoughtless and unkind. In the first place, you had no business playing with your Granny's hair. None whatsoever. Then you went and lost her hair, and compounded your shenanigans by being deceitful in trying to replace it."

As Pa continued, Red's knees began to steady. Pa was not going to whip them.

But by the time Pa finished, Red felt awful enough. He'd let Pa down. For punishment, Pa said, they were not allowed to play outside for the week. They'd do their chores, then stay inside. And they must apologize to Granny.

Red nodded, his head bowed. It was hard, but it was fair.

At suppertime, first Red, then Mac, apologized to their grandmother.

Granny's eyes crackled like ice. "I hope you gave them a right good whaling, Duncan."

"I dealt with them as I saw fit," said Pa, gently.

There was something in his tone that stopped even Granny. She subsided into offended silence, stabbing the odd angry glance at Red and even Mac.

It seemed like Mac was no longer the favourite; they were now equally in Granny's bad books. Somehow, Red didn't get a lot of satisfaction from it.

At first, everyone was too quiet. Almost like being at a funeral proper, instead of just watching the hearse go by. Ma made a few pleasant remarks to Granny but gave up when she remained silent.

Then Ellen asked Ma about the quilt pattern she'd borrowed, and Ma told Ellen about it, and how Dr. MacLeod had gone off to Sprucecliffe in a hurry because Annie Moore's baby had colic. When Ellen tutted, Ma said, her eyes twinkling, that it was likely no more than gas and she doubted the doctor would've been in such a hurry if Annie Moore wasn't such a dab hand at making the doctor's favourite raisin pie. Laughter spurted around the table and then the usual thrum of conversation filled the air.

Red gazed out the window as he ate his cold pork roast and leftover vegetables. The sun, skirting the tips of the spruces on the other side of the hollow, cast long shadows across the red and green stripes of the turnip field.

There were a powerful lot of things in this world he didn't understand.

A few weeks ago, in Sunday school, they'd read the story of Samson. How he'd lost all his strength when Delilah cut his hair.

What was so special about hair, anyway?

Red reached across for more cold pork and dared to look at Granny.

For a fleeting moment he saw how old she was. Her face was sad and wrinkled, her hair thin and grey. She wasn't that big, either. Not much bigger than him, come to think of it. She didn't really take up a lot of space at the table.

Red tried to understand what that switch had meant to her. He tried to imagine what it might be like to grow old. To have no home of your own and rotate among your children, maybe sometimes feeling like you didn't quite belong.

He felt a strange ache in his chest, like the feeling he got when he heard the last train whistle at night, plaintive and mourning.

Granny caught his glance and glared at him.

Red dropped his eyes. Then he made himself look back at her.

He waited to tell her he was really sorry. That she was

his grandmother, and a part of the family. That she had the right to be there, sitting around the table with them.

But he couldn't find the words.

All he could do was not look away.

BUNCH O' TROUBLE

UNCH WAS A PEST.

Red knew she was following him, even before he spied her short square body trailing after him down the dusty lane from their house to the road.

Bunch was a darn little pest. He'd never let Ma or Pa catch him saying that word, but it felt good to think it, because that's what she was.

He swung around. "For cryin' out loud, you're not coming!"

Bunch stopped. She was wearing that faded old pink dress that was much too small, and she held a pail in one hand and a pole in the other. Mac had cut that pole the last time they'd gone fishing, and it was ridiculously big for her.

Red let out a sputter of exasperation. He'd spent time with her yesterday, hadn't he? He'd made her that whirligig out of paper; you'd think that'd be enough.

Gripping his bucket and pole, he walked faster down the lane to Sprucecliffe Road, then began to run along it, past the fields. The hayfield was now bare with golden stubble interspersed with weeds, and the potato field sprawling with vines that were starting to yellow. He raced down the dip in the road and up by the neighbouring farms.

He could hear Bunch running after him.

"Bunch, you're not coming and that's that!"

It wasn't often Pa gave him a whole Saturday afternoon off, and for once he'd even finished his homework without Ellen around to make him do it over. Besides, September days didn't get much finer than this, and once school closed for the potato harvest, he'd be lucky to have time to spit between sun-up and sundown.

Red hesitated as he neared the deserted McKinley house up on the hill, to his right. Bunch wouldn't dare follow if he cut through that yard. The house had buckled walls, a tilted roof and glass-less windows; it looked like a twisted, gaping face with blind eyes. Shoulder-high grass crouched around it, along with goldenrod and other weeds.

He didn't really believe it was haunted, but his stomach curled at the thought of cutting through there.

Sticking to the road, Red sprinted by the house. Just a couple of days ago, Gooley had told him how his younger brother thought everyone who died ended up as ghosts in that house. He and Gooley had cracked up laughing about it, but still . . .

Red crossed the fallow field on the other side of the McKinley house to Shea's wood trail. It was dancing with leaf-dappled sunshine, and Gooley waited partway up, with his rod and pail.

"What's she doing?" asked Gooley. His sandy lashes blinked up and down.

"For the last time, Bunch," said Red, "you're not coming!" He wasn't about to spend his one free afternoon watching out for her.

Bunch stopped, her sturdy legs planted on the trail, her face set in that determined scowl.

Red shook his head in disgust. What could you do with a sister who didn't say anything, but just kept being determined?

"Yaaaah!" Red rushed towards her. "Shoo! Git!"

Bunch stood her ground. When she got determined, Bunch was awfully hard to move.

"Go home, Tiddlywinks!" yelled Red.

Bunch scowled harder, but Red saw her flush.

Ha, that got her! Uncle Hec called all little girls *Tiddlywinks* because he could never remember their names; it always made Bunch madder'n a wet hen.

"Tiddlywinks, Tiddlywinks, Tiddlywinks!"

"I'm not Tiddlywinks!" shouted Bunch, goaded into talking.

"Tiddlywinks, Tiddlywinks, Tiddlywinks!" Red circled around her.

"You stop that!" cried Bunch.

Gooley caught on and began to run around her too, calling, "Tiddly-piddly-widdly-winks!"

"Stop that!" Bunch scooped up a handful of dirt and threw it at Red.

"Ha-ha! Missed me. Missed me, Tiddlywinks."

Red paused as Bunch's eyes filled with tears. He didn't mean to make her cry—but he sure as heck didn't want her tagging along, for all that.

"Tiddlywinks!" he shouted one last time, for emphasis.

Bunch's face puckered. She picked up a stone and heaved it at Red.

It grazed the side of his head.

Red put his hand to his temple. She'd hit him! She'd actually hit him!

He squinted at Bunch.

She stood frozen, her eyes big, mouth open.

"A hit, a hit!" hollered Gooley. He made shooting noises.

Red turned to Gooley. He dropped his bucket and pole and staggered around. He bent over double and reeled.

Bunch let out a strangled scream.

Red almost fell down, then dragged himself up and lurched about some more. He trembled and shook.

"You killed him! Killed him dead!" cried Gooley.

Red let his knees give way, slowly, slowly, then dropped to the ground. It was his best dying yet . . . but where was Mac when it counted?

He lay still, eyes closed. He heard footsteps. Rapid breathing.

"Red?" It was Bunch.

Red lay still, trying not to laugh.

"Red!" She shook him. "You awright?"

He was about to jump up with a *boo,* then he suddenly realized—if he stayed dead, Bunch might just go away.

Gooley must have thought the same thing.

"He's done for, Bunch." Gooley's voice sounded scared. "You killed him. Your Ma's going to be awful mad."

Bunch gasped. Red felt her hands shaking him. "Red, wake up! I didn't mean it. I'm sorry, Red."

He couldn't let her cry like that!

But before he could get up, Gooley pressed him down.

"Move 'way, Bunch. Let me check his breath. That's how you tell if they're dead."

Red played along and held his breath.

"Nope," said Gooley. "He's not breathin'. I guess he's a goner." Gooley practically sat on Red to hold him still.

For a moment there was silence. Then Red heard

wailing, and footsteps running away. The crying got fainter and fainter.

At last, he dared to open one eye. Gooley's freckled face twinkled down at him. "Come on, let's get out of here."

Red sprang to his feet. There was no sign of Bunch; she sure could run fast. That was a bit of a mean trick, but at least it got rid of her.

Gripping their poles and buckets, Red and Gooley raced down the sun-spotted wood trail and across the back of MacPherson's pasture field. Steering clear of the cows and horses, dodging cow patties, they bounded up the steep incline, onto the highest part of Dunvegan Road.

Red paused to look back. Way over to the left, across a patchwork of rolling fields—red, gold and shades of green—he could just make out their barns and the white gleam of their house. Beyond were more farms, their long, narrow fields interspersed with stretches of woods, and in the distance, the silver-blue glitter of the sea.

Thank goodness, there was no sign of Bunch.

"Come on!" cried Gooley.

They raced across the road and plunged into the wood trail on the other side. Deep in the woods, Red bent over to catch his breath.

"Think she'll come after?" asked Gooley.

"Nah, she doesn't know the way." Red straightened up. Bunch was probably home by now, crying to Ma. "You don't s'pose she really believes . . . ?"

Gooley made a scoffing sound. "She'd have to be dumber than a sack of hammers to believe it. Come on, we'd best get movin' before she comes back . . ."

Laughing and shoving, they raced down the twisting path, through a stand of dense spruce, then mixed hardwood trees, until at last they came down to the creek.

"Ssshh!" said Red. "Quiet now. Fish."

Gooley nodded.

Red's back eased as he settled into the serious business of fishing. The creek was long and curved, with slender white birches mixed with maples on Red's side, and dark-green spruce on the other. He and Gooley sat in their usual place under a few maples, by a deep hole in the creek. That maple shade felt some good. They baited their hooks with worms and let the lines dangle into the water. Red had cut the perfect birch tree for his pole, good and straight, with just the right give to it.

It was a grand afternoon. The fish bit and bit. Gooley caught eleven trout and Red caught nine, except, as Red pointed out, two of his fish were way bigger than Gooley's, so technically, pound for pound, he had more fish. They hung their fish by the gills onto forked switches and, arguing all the way, headed down a ways to another part of the creek where there was a wider hole, good and deep for swimming.

"One, two, three!" They jumped in.

Red floated on his back, spouting water. Gooley tried spouting too, but Red's spout was way higher, so Gooley dived down and pulled Red under. Red sputtered and gasped, and gave chase. Gooley came up laughing, and then they tried to see who could hold his breath longest underwater, and Gooley won, like he always did.

At last, when their hands and feet were wrinkled like prunes, they headed out of the water.

Mosquitoes began to swarm around them.

"Boy, they're somethin' fierce." Red swatted as he pulled on his shirt. With the warm weather they'd been having, the mosquitoes hadn't been dying off as usual. But it must have been later in the day than he'd thought if they were so thick. "Come on, I've got to get back."

Gooley shrugged. As far as Red was concerned, Gooley had it pretty easy. His father ran the store on Berryfield Road, and Gooley never had any regular chores because his older brothers and sisters milked the cows and tended their twenty acres for hay and pasture. The family even had extra help that summer because Gooley's two hulking big cousins from the Boston States were staying with them.

One time, when Ellen was fresh home from college, she'd said, all sniffy and superior, that there was no such place as the Boston States, and that the correct name was the New England States. Ma had turned to her, with a glint in her eye that looked alarmingly like Cat-less Granny's, and said that everyone on the Island always called them the Boston States, and if it was good enough for her and Pa, it should be good enough for Ellen, unless Ellen thought she was too good for them.

Swatting mosquitoes and some blackflies, Red and Gooley made their way back through the woods and pasture field to Shea's wood trail. Gooley complained about how his two cousins snored at night and ate too much. Things might be bad in the Boston States, he said, but why should his uncle send his boys over just so's he could save on food, and let Gooley's Pa be eaten out of house and home? But when Gooley'd said that to his Pa, his Pa had cuffed him and said he wouldn't tolerate anyone in his house acting so inhospitable, and blood was thicker than water. Gooley said that made no sense because what did blood or water have to do with it, and he just wanted his share of the trout he'd caught instead of his cousins eating the lot.

Partway down the trail, Gooley took his usual zigzag path between the fields to his own house behind the family store, while Red hurried along by the road. He wasn't about to cut across the McKinley lot, even though it was still broad daylight.

Red raced home and flung open the porch screen door. Ma was in the kitchen proper. The stove had been moved back in there a couple of weeks ago when the nights had turned chilly—Pa always had it in place by the first day of autumn.

"Ma, look! I got nine big 'uns. Gooley caught eleven, but I got more pound for pound."

Ma, wrapped in her gingham apron, turned from rolling out biscuit dough. "My, those are fine and fat fellas." Her face beamed. "Put them on the block, Red. I'll clean 'em and fry 'em up for supper. It'll be a right treat. The leftover ham can keep 'til tomorrow."

Red's stomach growled. No one fried up trout quite like Ma. He was hungry enough to eat the bottom out of an iron pot.

"Now go and help Pa with the chores," said Ma, cutting out rounds of biscuit dough and putting them on the baking tray. "But wash up first. And *properly*. We don't need any sus*fish*ious smells." She tilted her head towards the sitting room, where Granny sat with Ellen.

Red grinned and nodded. If there was the slightest smell of fish about him, Cat-less Granny would be sure to sniff it out, and make him wash all over.

Red dipped up water from the tank by the stove and scrubbed at the basin, then pulled on his boots to go to the barns.

"Oh, Red," called out Ma. "Tell Bunch to come inside and get washed."

Bunch. Red had forgotten about her.

He glanced about outside, but there was no sign of her, not by the wellhouse or the barns. He went to the front of the house, but Bunch wasn't on the lawn or under the fruit trees. Likely she was playing with the cats in the little barn.

He'd find her later. She might still be mad.

But at least he'd had his afternoon without watching out for her.

In the big barn, Mac was milking his third cow. "Took long enough, didn't you?" he muttered. "Pa's out there filling the water trough."

"Sorry. The fish bit and then we went for a swim." Red took the tippy stool to milk the last cow. "You should've come, instead of porin' over your books."

He was pretty fed up with Mac acting all serious and superior, just because he'd started Latin and French in school. Mac said he had to study hard to get into college, but he wouldn't be going for at least another two years. And if Alex decided to go on to university to get his degree, Mac would have to wait yet another year before Alex would be able to pay for him.

When they finished, Red said, "You take the milk in to Ma. I'll take the cows back to pasture and clean the stalls." It was the least he could do. "And tell Bunch Ma wants her inside." Better let Mac find Bunch, in case she was still sore.

Whistling, Red led the cows back to the pasture, then quickly shovelled out the cow droppings in the stalls; it never took long this time of year. He helped Pa carry buckets of water from the wellhouse to the trough in the pasture. When Flash came nickering up to the gate, Red shut it quickly, wary of the evil glint in Flash's eye.

Red sauntered back to the house. Near the woodshed, he saw Clover and Tubbs snapping up the fish entrails Ma had thrown out for them. She was some quick cleaning the fish—it would have taken him forever. Red pumped an extra bucket of water at the wellhouse and carried it to the back porch. He knew Ma would insist he wash with soap again.

All that washing had to be bad for him; Chirpy Carmichael, one of the older boys who rarely came to school, said you pretty well needed some dirt to protect you from germs. When Chirpy was younger and had come to school regularly, the teacher had written to his parents to say that he needed a bath because he smelled bad. Chirpy's Pa had written back, "Your job is to learn 'em, not smell 'em." But Ma said if she ever caught Red looking or smelling like Chirpy, she'd learn *him* by dunking him in the water trough and scrubbing him with a horse brush.

As he went into the back porch Ma glanced up and motioned him to the basin. "Where's Bunch? Did you tell her to come in?"

"Mac's doing that," said Red.

"She trouble you any?" asked Ma, dipping the fish in flour.

"What? I mean, pardon?"

"Bunch. Did she trouble you when you were fishing?"

Red avoided Ma's eyes. "She didn't come with us. She just took off."

"Did she now?"

Red felt Ma's quick, piercing glance on the back of his neck. If Cat-less Granny hadn't been nearby, Red knew Ma might have questioned him, maybe even given him a tongue-lashing. Having Granny around was useful at times.

"Wonder where she got to, then," said Ma, rolling another fish in the flour and shaking off the extra. "Haven't seen hide nor hair of her all afternoon."

Mac came clattering through the screen door. "Bunch here?" he asked. "Didn't see her in the yard."

Ma clicked her tongue. "That child. Wandering off, getting up to goodness knows what." She called through to the sitting room, "Ellen. Is Bunch upstairs? Can you look?"

"I was just there, Ma," said Ellen, eyes fixed on the lace she was tatting. "And I didn't see her."

"Boys, go and find her right away. Supper'll be ready soon, and dear knows, we must be punctual." Ma's eyes flickered towards the sofa, where Granny sat.

Red dried his hands and went outside with Mac.

"You check the hayloft," said Red. "I'll look around the henhouse." Red knew Bunch wouldn't be there. She didn't much like the hens, because that big rooster always made for her.

Red ambled down the track between the barns to the henhouse, checked it, then jumped over the fence to the pasture. He looked down the back of the barns and across the field to the trees by the fence, then went over to the big willow, where Bunch sometimes liked to play. She wasn't there. The cows stared at him calmly, then went back to chewing cud.

Red jogged back. The heat of the day was giving way to a cooler breeze as the sun cast longer shadows. In the little barn, Red checked around the buggy, the working wagon, the light driving wagon and the sleigh, as well as the binder and other farm equipment. The cats were in there, snoozing after their feast, but no sign of Bunch.

Red went outside and over to the workshop at the other end of the little barn, even though he knew Bunch wouldn't dare go there. Pa had made it clear he wouldn't tolerate her being anywhere near the saws and tools. She wasn't there either.

Where was she? Red scratched a blackfly bite behind his ear. Ma was always telling Bunch to let her know where she was going, but Bunch hardly ever did.

As he left the workshop, Mac came out of the big barn. "She's not in the hayloft," he called.

"What about the lilacs behind the vegetable garden?"

"I looked," said Mac. "Did you check under the big willow?"

"She's not there."

Mac blinked hard. "Then where is she? She's never this hard to find."

A cold, delicate finger pressed into Red's chest. Surely Bunch couldn't have thought . . . ? Nah!

Bunch wasn't stupid. She could be a pest at times, but in no way was she stupid. Why, she'd known her letters and numbers even before she'd started school last year. And when she'd been only three and a half she'd taken off for school one day, all by herself, eager to learn. The teacher had made Red take her back home, and Ma had been in a state, searching for Bunch.

Bunch was probably just hiding someplace.

Ma came out the back porch door. "Did you find her?"

Red and Mac shook their heads.

"Find who?" asked Pa, coming up to the wellhouse.

"Bunch." Ma, let her breath out in an exasperated puff. "Can't imagine where that child's got to. I'll have to give her another good talking-to about wandering off."

"She can't be far, Kathleen," said Pa. "Did you check the little barn? The hayloft?"

"Boys, did you look?" asked Ma.

Mac and Red nodded.

"Why don't I go look again," said Pa.

"Red," said Ma. "Go and check the cellar. She shouldn't be down there, she can't abide the place, but just in case . . ."

Red nodded. He lit a candle and hurried down the stone steps. "Bunch," he called. "You here?"

Shadows leapt with his guttering candle as Red searched the empty cellar. It smelled fresh and clean this time of year, not like the heavy turnip smell of mid-winter, when it smelled like stale old fart. Soon, the cellar would be filled again with the new crops of potatoes and turnips, but for now there were just two small piles from last year's crops in the corner. It didn't take long to see that Bunch wasn't down there. Red lifted the old pail that Pa hadn't got around to mending, in case, by some freak chance, Bunch had managed to squeeze under it.

Ma stood at the top of the cellar steps, the lines of her chin hard from the tightness of her mouth. "Well?"

Red shook his head. He spat on his fingers and put out the candle.

He wasn't scared. Bunch was bound to show up any minute. But his stomach kept diving, the same way it did when he went past the old McKinley house.

Red rushed past Granny in the sitting room, unmindful of her tutting, and sprinted upstairs. He searched the room Bunch shared with Ellen—she'd had to give up her own small room to Cat-less Granny—then Granny's room, then Ma and Pa's room, and even the loft, and under the beds. He peered out the loft window, scanning Ma's vegetable garden, across the side field, now dull green with heavy, straggly turnips, then over to the hollow. Bunch would never go to the hollow on her own, would she? She was afraid of the place.

When he came down again, Pa was in the kitchen, rubbing the back of his neck. "Well, she's not in the barns or the stable. Nor in the workshop. I looked everywhere."

Ma's forehead puckered.

Granny trotted over from the sofa, her knitting needles in hand, along with some muddy purple yarn. "I don't mean to worry you, Kathleen, but remember over in Geary how that little MacDermott girl went wandering off into the swamp? They never found her until—"

"Please, Ma, that's not helpful!" said Ma.

Granny soured her mouth but mercifully kept silent. Red knew Ma must be real worried to speak so sharply to Granny.

"There's no swamp around here," said Pa. He turned to Red. "You say she didn't go with you."

Red shook his head. Now wasn't the time to explain, except . . .

"I . . . well . . . I discouraged her from coming," he said.

Ma clicked her tongue.

Red swallowed, then forced out the words, "But if she tried to follow us into in the woods, she might have . . . she might have got lost." His heart began to thud uncomfortably, now that he'd said it aloud.

"Oh, Duncan." Ma's freckles stood out darkly as her skin went pale. "What if she is lost?"

Pa brushed his square hand across his forehead. "We'd best get searching. If she's in the woods, we have to find her before dark." Calmly, Pa told Mac to get Callum MacMillan, their neighbour on one side, and Red to get Joshua Munn, their neighbour on the other side. "Tell Joshua to call the store and get a search party going. Tell them to bring lanterns. If it gets dark before we find her, we'll need them."

In a daze, Red raced along the back of the house, then between the turnip field and the back hay field, down past the Munns' potato field, pasture and vegetable patch to their house. He burst into the kitchen without even knocking.

Mr. and Mrs. Munn and their three boys were eating supper around the kitchen table. Red panted out his story and Mr. Munn, a short, wiry man, got up at once. Henry, the oldest, who was seventeen and near as wide as he was tall, went to get some rope and a lantern. Tommy, who was as thin as a drink of water, also got up. He was only Mac's age, but he always acted snotty and superior because he'd quit school a couple of years back to work on the farm.

"By the jumpin' Moses," said Mrs. Munn. "Whatever next! Git along, Joshua. Git along, boys. Not you, Clarence," she said to the youngest. "Be more trouble'n you're worth. Hush now! Don't need no backtalk from you. Red, tell your Ma I'll be over, soon's I can. I'll call the store, and git folks rounded up to help." The Munns had one of the few telephones in the village.

Red raced back home. He felt like there was a stone in his chest ten times bigger than the one Bunch had thrown at him.

What if she *had* tried to follow him into the woods?

What if she'd come back to the wood trail, seen that he'd gone, and been all mad, but still determined? Bunch was some determined when she took the notion. And if she'd been out there in the woods the whole time that he and Gooley had been fishing and swimming, and she still hadn't found them, then she must be good and lost.

Those woods were deep, and criss-crossed with

trails. Red could never keep straight which part of the woods belonged to which farmer. Pa was always saying to mind the wood trail you took, so you could find your way back out. He and Gooley had nearly got lost more than once and they knew those woods. Bunch was just a little girl.

The stone in his chest turned, scraping his heart.

Back at the house, people began to gather for the search. Ma, her face tightly calm, her eyes blazing, told them what had happened. Gooley and his brothers came from the store along with their Pa, Mr. MacKenzie. Gooley's two burly cousins from the Boston States insisted on coming too. Mr. Munn muttered that he couldn't imagine what good they'd be, seeing as how they didn't know their way around, and if they went and got their fool selves lost, he wasn't about to go searchin' for *them.*

Gooley tugged Red aside, his pale eyelashes blinking fast. "You didn't tell anyone about . . . you know."

Red shook his head and turned away. He hadn't told, but to have Gooley ask made him feel like there was a mess of worms squirming inside his stomach.

When the search parties set out, Red went along with Mr. Munn, Henry and Tommy to search the woods where he'd been fishing earlier.

The mosquitoes and blackflies seemed to be out searching too as Red and the Munns scoured the woods.

Calling Bunch's name, they went all the way to the creek where Red and Gooley had fished, then to the swimming hole. Red's heart sank as the sun dipped lower. It would be dark soon.

At last they stopped, a little way past the swimming hole. Even in the dimming light, Red could see how worried Mr. Munn looked. "She wouldn't have tried to go swimmin' on her own, would she?"

"We swam for quite a while. She wasn't here, then."

Mr. Munn slapped flies off the back of his neck. "Well, can yer think of anyplace else she mighta got to?"

Red shook his head. He couldn't go crying, not in front of the Munns.

Mr. Munn put his hand on Red's shoulder. "Steady, now, lad. Likely as not she's already been found. And if not, me and the boys'll get lanterns and keep lookin'. All night if we has to. Don't you go frettin', we'll find her. But we'd best git back now, and tell your Pa."

Henry Munn clumsily patted Red, and even Tommy made soothing sounds. Normally, Tommy lost few opportunities to scoff at Mac and Red for being all soft and sissy, going to school instead of working on the farm.

Red followed the Munns as they traced their way back along the dimming wood trail. At the crest of Dunvegan Road, Red stopped to look around, eyes straining.

The fields were shrouded in the fading light. Lamplight glowed from the windows of a few farmhouses. The sea on the horizon was a dark line, with the tips of spruces etched like knives against the dusky pearl sky. Soon, it would be as black as the inside of a cow.

Red shivered. His familiar, easy world suddenly seemed strange and dangerous. A terrible place you could get lost in.

Bunch must be so scared. What would it be like, being that small and alone?

A crisp breeze had sprung up by the time they reached Shea's wood trail. It put off some of the mosquitoes and blackflies, but Red knew it would be chilly soon. It always cooled off nights, and this was September. Bunch had been in her bare feet and wearing that short old pink dress that Ma had been wanting to cut up long and ever ago for the rug she was hooking, except Bunch wouldn't let her.

Red put on a spurt and raced down the wood trail ahead of the Munns, suddenly frantic to get home. Maybe Mr. Munn was right—maybe someone had found Bunch by now. Red sprinted along the road, past the McKinley house, down the dip and up again towards his house.

In the distance, he saw lanterns bobbing and hurried over.

One look at Pa's grim face and he knew they hadn't found Bunch. Others had checked the woods back of the farm, all through the hollow, the station, and even along Berryfield Road. When the Munns caught up, they began to talk to Pa about where to look next.

In a daze, Red went home and slipped into the back porch. A crowd of folks bustled about in the kitchen. Red glimpsed Maisie Munn pouring boiling water into the teapot, a mess of cups and mugs on the table, and Granny's lips moving a mile a minute, along with her knitting needles. Ma, her arms wrapped around herself, stood at the side window, her eyes too bright, like they were trying to penetrate the dark.

Red picked up the small lantern. He lit it with shaking fingers and headed off down the lane again.

Where could Bunch be?

He went over it again, him on the ground, Bunch crying.

It washed over him what she might have felt. Scared. Lonely. Maybe even terrified.

Where would she go? She'd been wailing as she ran away, "Sorry, Red. Sorry, Red."

Red stopped.

She couldn't.

She couldn't have thought she'd really killed him.

With a chill, he remembered a couple of days back at the supper table. Red had repeated that story about Gooley's little brother thinking that everyone who died ended up as ghosts in the McKinley house. They'd all laughed, but Bunch's eyes had gone bigger and bigger, until Ma had said, "Enough of that foolishness. Such nonsense." Then Granny had told off Red for talking with a speck of food in his mouth . . .

Bunch wouldn't believe that crazy yarn, would she? She couldn't! She was as smart as a bee.

At the end of the lane, Red hovered at the edge of a group of men with lanterns talking to Pa. He saw Ma's tall body tightly silhouetted at the window, like she was holding herself in.

Red slipped away. His lantern jerked and bobbed, casting nervous pools of light as he headed down Sprucecliffe Road, back in the direction he'd taken earlier with the Munns. He hurried down the dip in the road, fingers of ghostly air brushing against him, then up the other side.

Heart pounding, he stopped outside the McKinley house.

It was all lopsided, that house, with empty windows like the eye sockets of a skull. The slanted door looked like the mouth of an old person, open in a wail. In the daylight it was strange enough, but in this fading light it felt . . . actively hostile.

Waiting.

A wind came up. The branches of the big maple tree scratched and creaked against the roof.

Hands shaking, Red started up the tangled lane to the

house. Monster weeds swayed, ready to pounce.

What if there *were* ghosts inside? What if . . . ?

Red turned and fled back to the road.

He couldn't do it. He just couldn't. His knees felt like water.

But—what if Bunch *was* in there?

Red looked again at the house.

He drew in a long, shuddering breath.

Then, putting his head down so he couldn't see anything, he ran along the lane straight to the front door.

It was ajar. What was that sound?

His heart.

His heart was going to burst.

Red tried to call out. But no sound came, except a squeak.

He tried again. "Bunch?"

Red began to turn away, then stopped.

Had he heard something? Something . . . moving inside?

His whole body went cold.

"Bunch?" His voice shook as he pulled at the door. It wailed and screeched.

"Bunch," shouted Red, trying to drown all the other sounds. "It's me, Red. Come on out, if you're in there."

He heard a little cry. Red yanked the door wide and went inside, holding the lantern high.

"Bunch? That you?"

A squeal from the pile of boards in the dark corner.

Red rushed over, brushing through loops of cobwebs.

Bunch cowered, half-covering her eyes. "I didn't mean to kill you, Red. I'm sorry, sorry . . ." She let out a shriek as he came closer.

Red put down the lantern and grabbed Bunch, hugging her.

Bunch fought and squirmed, but he held her, shouting, "I'm not dead, Bunch, I'm alive. See, I'm warm, I'm breathing. I didn't mean for you to think I was really dead."

Bunch stopped struggling. At last, she looked up. In the lantern's dim light, Red saw her dirty, tear-stained face.

"I'm sorry, Bunch. That was a mean trick. I never thought you'd . . ." Red's voice strangled as the knot in his throat tightened.

Bunch held still. Then her fists pounded his chest, his neck, and his face. Red didn't even put up his hands to defend himself.

He let her hit him. He wished she could hit harder.

At last, with a sob, Bunch stopped.

Red picked her up. Holding her tight—she was heavy, Bunch—he grabbed the lantern.

"Come on. Let's go home."

The floorboards creaked and moaned as he hurried out the door. Red's arms screamed with Bunch's weight, but he was not going to put her down.

"She's here. I found her!" he shouted, stumbling down the road. But the others were still too far to hear.

Bunch struggled against his arms and wriggled down.

He tried to take her hand but she shook it off and ran from him.

For a moment he felt a ghost of what she must have felt like when he hadn't let her come with him.

Red ran after her, shouting, "Pa, Ma. She's here. Bunch is here."

A scattering of lanterns came leaping towards them. Then Bunch was in Ma's arms. Ma was crying, and Pa was hugging them both.

"Where were you, pet?" Ma wiped Bunch's cheek, then her own. "Oh, I could just shake you . . ." Ma squeezed her tight.

"Where did you find her?" asked Pa.

"In the McKinley house."

"The McKinley house?" said Ma. "What in the world were you doing there, Honey-Bunch?"

In the sudden silence, Bunch looked at Red.

Red looked back, waiting.

Then Bunch said, "Nothing."

Red's lips shook. He knew he couldn't let it rest there.

He had to tell Pa.

Callum MacMillan, who was tall and bony, with straight brown hair and calm brown eyes, let out a deep sigh. "You folks go on home, now. I'll tell the others we found her." He ruffled Bunch's hair.

As Ma led the way back home with Bunch, Red tugged on Pa's sleeve.

"What is it, boy?"

"I've got to talk to you, Pa."

Pa looked at him and stopped. "I'm guessing you've got something to get off your chest?" In the lantern light, his eyes were as steady and kind as ever.

Red nodded.

Stumbling, trying not to cry, Red told him everything.

When he finished, Pa sighed. "Come on, let's get back. Your Ma's waiting."

They walked in silence.

Then Pa said, looking straight ahead, "I don't think you need me to punish you any. I'm guessin' you've been punished enough already." He put his hand on Red's shoulder.

The storm in Red's head began to settle. But something in his chest felt worse than if Pa had punished him. It seemed like that stone he'd been carrying had shattered into hundreds of sharper shards.

That night in bed, Red thought it over and decided that for the next week, and until after the potato harvest, he wouldn't play outside. Thank goodness, at least Cat-less Granny had announced that she was soon going to Aunt Nettie's, over in Nova Scotia, and then to Uncle Mac's in the Boston States. She couldn't abide the cold of the Maritime winters, even though she'd lived on the Island most of her life and all her children had been born there.

• • •

School shut down at the end of September and into early October, for the two weeks of potato harvest. Red was busier than a blue-bottomed fly, helping Pa harvest and bag potatoes. Everyone pitched in, Ma, Ellen and Bunch, and even Granny, who took over a good bit of the cooking. It was back-breaking work, and Red was just wiped each night.

Right after the potato harvest Granny left, and it seemed like everyone's spirits lifted. Clover and Tubbs were allowed back in the house, to Bunch's delight, and Ma's step was springier, and her old spark back. When Callum MacMillan stopped by, Ma took out the package of trick gum and casually offered him some. How they roared with laughter, Callum most of all, when the trick gum snapped at his fingers.

Then it was back to school, with homework each

night, and Ellen riding him harder than ever. She was crankier than usual because she'd had yet another fight with Stewart.

The first Saturday after school restarted was bright and sunny, unusually warm for October. Pa had even let the cows and horses out to pasture, but Red knew there wouldn't be many more days like this. In the morning, he, Mac and Pa, along with a few other local farmers, loaded bags of potatoes onto a freight car for the train going out west to help starving farmers on the Prairies.

Then, in the afternoon, while Mac studied, Red helped Pa put new shingles on the henhouse.

They were near done when Pa said, "Go on, boy. You've been working hard. Take the rest of the afternoon off." He smiled. "Go fishing."

Red hesitated. Did he deserve to go fishing?

Pa nodded.

Red whooped. It would likely be his last chance to fish this year. He sped down the lane and over to MacKenzie's store at the crossroads, found Gooley, and arranged to meet him on Shea's wood trail. Gooley could always be counted on to go fishing.

Red raced back home to get his fishing gear, his heart hooting and hollering with the colours of the trees around him—red, copper, orange and a yellow so piercing it was like the sun itself.

As he sprinted up the lane, he saw Bunch sitting under an apple tree, playing with her dolls, and Clover and Tubbs. Red stopped.

He scratched his head, then said casually, "I'm going fishing. With Gooley. You can come if you want."

Bunch looked at him from under her brows. It was how Pa looked at you before giving you a talking-to. But she said nothing.

Red sighed. He used the privy, got his fishing gear, told Ma where he was going, then pulled on his rubber boots and hurried down the road. If it weren't for the colour of the trees, and the October look of the fields—most of them bare with red furrowed soil or with golden stubble and green weeds, and a few others ratty with turnips, waiting to be pulled after a hard frost—Red might've thought it was still summer, it was so warm. He rushed past the McKinley house to Shea's wood trail where Gooley waited, with his rod and pail in hand.

"Come on!" Gooley shouted.

Red started to run when something made him stop and half-turn.

He saw a short, squat figure a good way behind.

Gooley's blue eyes looked past Red, then back at him. "Is she comin'?"

Red hooked his thumbs around his suspenders and waited until Bunch was within earshot. "You comin'?"

Bunch stopped. And scowled.

Red let his breath out in a long gust, then turned and began to walk on.

From the corner of his eye, he saw Bunch still trundling after them.

He pulled on Gooley's arm to slow him down, and began to whistle.

PURE AGGRAVATION

AGGRAVATION," SAID ELLEN. *Tap, tap, tap* went her toe against the wooden schoolroom floor.

"Aggravation," repeated Red, playing for time. He licked his lips and squinted at his sister. "A. G. R—"

"Wrong!" snapped Ellen. The look she gave him said, *Wait 'til we get home.*

Pete was next in line. "Aggravation," said Ellen.

"Aggravation," said Pete. He scrunched up his eyes and, with scarcely a pause for breath, rattled off, "A-g-g-r-a-v-a-t-i-o-n."

"Correct," said Ellen. "Go up one."

As Pete moved to the head of the line, Ellen gave Red another scorching glance, as if to say that if Pete could do it, Red ought to do it too, and better, for being the teacher's brother.

Red had studied.

Some.

After supper the night before, he and Pa had gone to the workshop to sort out the hardwood boards they'd need for the tobacco caddies they made each winter for Morrison's store. Supplying those caddies got them their credit at the store, so Pa was awfully particular to make them with good hardwood, and precisely six by six by five inches, for the chewing-tobacco plugs that would fill them.

When they were done, Red had lingered behind, meaning to go right back to the house to study—but that spare bit of maple had just about cried out to be picked up. Before he knew it, the new milking stool was half made, and Mac was looking for him, and he had to hurry indoors and try to learn those words before bedtime.

Why did that word need two *g*'s anyway? You'd think one would be enough for any sensible word.

By the time the spelling bee was over, Red was near the bottom of the line. Only Chirpy Carmichael was below him, and Chirpy only ever came to school to rest up from farm work and annoy his Pa, who didn't see any point in highfalutin education.

As Red went down the aisle to his seat, Mac, who sat at the back with the oldest pupils, gave him a sympathetic grimace.

Red flushed and fixed his eye on the pot-bellied stove near the back of the class. It wasn't Mac he minded looking foolish in front of. Slipping into his seat next to Gooley, Red glanced across the aisle and down a ways.

Shona Murray's head was bent over her text. Her hand played over and over with the end of her thick brown braid.

There was something about Shona's blue eyes and those dark, curly eyelashes . . . he'd never seen ones that curled like that. She was a year and a half younger than Red, and new to the school, but already one of the smartest girls. She was always well dressed and neat, too, for all her family lived in that shack back of the mill, where her Pa worked. Red often wondered what her house had been like in Detroit—her family had lived there before Mr. Murray lost his automobile factory job, because of the Depression. Had it been rich and fancy? Did she think the Applecross boys were beneath her?

She never seemed to notice him.

For once, Red was glad of it.

He jumped as Ellen smacked her ruler against the desk.

"Grade Six, open your arithmetic books to page thirty-seven. Do sums eight through twenty-five." She glanced stonily at Pud Hodgkins, who groaned. "Grade Five, open your geography books . . ."

Gooley whispered, "What's she so grumpy for?"

Ellen turned to Gooley. "No talking means no talking. Do you not understand this simple rule, Graham?"

Gooley nodded and shrank down in his seat.

"Sit up! No slouching," said Ellen.

Gooley sat up.

Red locked his eyes on his book. Ellen had always been strict, but for the past few weeks, ever since her last fight with Stewart, she'd been . . . well, pure aggravating. With four g's!

When Ellen let them out for recess, Red ran out into the thin November sunshine with the other boys. They raced across the frost-brown grass, around the side of the schoolhouse and up the sloping yard.

"What's the matter with your sister, anyway?" grumbled Gooley, tossing a ball up and down. "She's awful cross lately."

Red kicked a tuft of brown grass. He wasn't about to discuss his sister, not even with Gooley. Anyway, it was a mystery to him why Ellen and Stew kept fighting then getting back together. You'd think they'd make up their minds one way or the other, and stick to it.

"Yah," said Eddie Burke, sucking in his breath. He had a small, thin face with a crooked nose that had been broken in a fight. "She's got to be a regular crank." Eddie had got into trouble with Ellen for not knowing the exports of Sweden.

Red felt his neck go hot. It was one thing to say Ellen was cross, but another thing to call her a crank. He pretended not to hear.

Eddie swiped the back of his hand across his nose and stared defiantly at Red. "That's what she is, all right—a mean ol' crank." His scrappy body tensed for a fight.

Gooley turned to Red as if to say, *Well?*

"Don't go callin' my sister names," said Red.

"Guess I can call the teacher any name I want," said Eddie. "Your sister is a crank, a mean ol'—"

Red tackled him.

"Fight, fight!" cried someone.

Entangled in a flurry of fists, Red was only distantly aware of girls screaming. Next thing he knew he was on top of Eddie, yelling, "Take it back. Take it back!"

Then someone gripped his shoulder and dragged him off.

Ellen.

She yanked Eddie to his feet.

"Boys! For shame! I do not permit fighting in my schoolyard. Inside, right now. Eddie, for mercy's sake, wipe your nose."

Ellen marched them back to the schoolhouse. She drew two small circles on the chalkboard and the boys had to stand with their noses pressed against them. Red's circle was just low enough that he had to stoop the whole hour. The injustice of it galled worse than his aching back. He knew Ellen would be sure to bring it up at home, and Ma and Pa would ask why he'd been fighting—and he wouldn't be able to say anything.

When school was over, Red gathered his books and pulled the strap tight around them. He saw Shona laughing with a couple of other girls. Were they laughing about him?

He rushed to the porch and grabbed his cap and coat, nearly knocking over the bucket of drinking water brought over each morning from the farm across the road. He sprinted out the door, across the yard to Dunvegan Road, down a ways, then cut through a bare field, all stubble and weeds, onto Sprucecliffe Road.

Mac caught up with him alongside the old McKinley house.

"Don't mind Ellen," puffed Mac. "She doesn't mean anything—"

"Who asked you?" said Red.

Mac bumped into him. Red bumped back, harder.

Then they were shoving each other, and Mac cried, "Race you!"

Red put on a burst of speed and reached the porch door just before Mac. Panting and laughing, he dashed into the kitchen.

The sharp, scratching smell of lye etched all the way

up his nose. Aunt Lina was at the table, stirring the contents of a big cast-iron pot, with Ma beside her. The window was open to let out the fumes. Aunt Lina was one of Ma's cousins from Clearwater, and she always came over to help make the soap they used for washing clothes, and for scrubbing up when they came in from the barns.

She looked up, her round face glowing, her dark hair limp with sweat. "There you are, me young tadpoles! Here, Kathleen. Keep stirrin." She handed Ma the spoon, then wiped her hands on her apron and came over to give Mac and Red a hug.

"How was school today, boys?" Ma brushed her sleeve against her damp forehead.

"All right," said Mac.

"How did you do in spelling? Did you go up or down?"

"Up," said Mac. "I got to the head."

Ma turned to Red. Her blue eyes seemed to look all the way inside him.

"Went down," muttered Red. Thank goodness Ellen took her time coming home with Bunch at the end of the school day; the last thing he needed right now was Ellen filling in the details.

"Guess I'd better go help Pa in the barn," he said.

"Wait a minute, me young tadpoles," said Aunt Lina. "I've got something to show yez before Ellen gets home."

She rummaged in her bag and pulled out a stiff rectangular card.

"This here is a greetin' card." Aunt Lina's eyes shone. "I got it from Angus over in the Boston States for m' birthday. He mus' be doin' some good to send a card like this."

Red stared at the pink card. It had a picture of a yellow basket overflowing with purple pansies. Written across the top was *Happy Birthday, Sister.*

"Your Ma and I was talkin' about Ellen's birthday comin' up," said Aunt Lina. "And how it's special, her being twenty-one and all. So I thought mebbe yez could give her this card, to mark the day."

Bewildered, Red looked from Aunt Lina's shining face to Ma's amused one.

"I guess they're a newfangled notion in big cities, these greeting cards," said Ma, stirring the lye and fat mixture.

"Yah!" said Aunt Lina, inhaling as she spoke. "To say happy birthday."

"But why should we give her a card to say happy birthday?" said Red. "We're right here, aren't we?"

"Yeah," said Mac. "We can say it in person."

"It's a special birthday, me young tadpoles," said Aunt Lina, shaking Red's shoulder. "Ellen can put it in her scrapbook to remember. Go on, open it up. Look inside.

I stuck a clean piece of paper over where Angus wrote, so it looks like new."

Red opened the card, with Mac peering over his shoulder.

On the top were more pansies and below, in fancy script, was written:

> *Birthday Greetings to a Wonderful Sister*
> *Your many kind and thoughtful ways,*
> *Your sweet and cheerful, smiling face*
> *Your soothing hands, your gentle words*
> *Make you the best sister in all the world.*

Aunt Lina had pasted a strip of bright pink paper at the bottom.

Red stared and stared at the words. They made him sort of queasy.

He twisted the card around, but the words looked no better upside down.

"Here." He shoved the card at Mac. "You give it to her."

"No. You give it." Mac shoved it back.

"Why should I?" said Red.

"Now boys," said Ma, glancing up from the pot. But her lips twitched with laughter.

Aunt Lina put one arm around Red and the other

around Mac. "No, no. It's for all of yez to give your sister. You can put Alex's name on it, too. I'm sure he'll like that."

"Yes, and write something of your own," said Ma, soothingly.

"But it's already got a lot of words in it," said Red. "I don't see—"

"Well, you can cross out a few if you want," said Ma. "And put in some of your own." She raised her eyebrows warningly, as if to say, *Enough.* Ma could never abide rudeness.

"Yah." Aunt Lina sucked in her breath. "Make the card special from yez fellas. Personal, like."

"All right." Mac shrugged. "I guess Ellen would like it. It's a pretty card. Thanks, Aunt Lina."

Red felt the knot in his back twist tighter. That was the trouble with Mac; he was entirely too easygoing. Red could hardly keep protesting now, all by himself, especially with Ma looking at him like that, and Aunt Lina acting so pleased.

"Thanks, Aunt Lina," said Red, at last.

"Put it away so Ellen doesn't see it when she gets home," said Ma. "And go help Pa. Supper's likely to be late; this soap's taking forever."

Red thrust the card between his school books, then he and Mac pulled on their overalls and rubber boots. Mac started on his usual tuneless whistle as they mucked out the barns. Red felt like tossing the dirty straw right in Mac's face.

When they sat down to supper later that evening, Red glanced at Ellen. He wondered when she'd light into him about the spelling bee and the fight.

Then Pa started to talk about the turnip crop. "I was over in Morrison's store in Clearwater and George Gillis was saying the price of turnips is dropping. I'm thinking we'd best get that crop out before the price plummets. George said Stew's already got his..." Pa's voice trailed off as Ma shook her head slightly.

George Gillis was Stewart Gillis's uncle. Stew's farm was right next to his.

Ellen looked down at her plate and began to cut her potato into smaller and smaller pieces.

Ma jumped in to talk about a new crochet pattern she'd got from Aunt Lina, and how, when Dora Parker and her little girl Mollie had dropped by, Mollie had asked if it was holy work, because the crochet was full of holes, and if that meant you could do it on Sundays.

They all laughed, but Ellen barely smiled.

"Eat up," said Ma, passing around the casserole dish. "It's going to the pigs anyway."

When Ma said that, Ellen usually looked at the boys and said, "Yes, two-legged pigs." But tonight she didn't even notice. She was quiet for the rest of the meal.

Red finished his pumpkin pie, hardly daring to believe that Ellen had forgotten to bring up what had happened in school. Part of him was relieved, but part of him wished he could cheer her up. Ellen looked so . . . so flat without her usual snap. That must have been some fight she'd had with Stew. He'd never stayed away this long before.

After the supper dishes had been cleared, Red, Mac and Bunch began to study at the table by the bright glow of the Aladdin mantle lamp, with the cats curled around their feet. Ellen sat with them, planning her lessons for the next day. Ma drilled Bunch first with her spelling, and then Red.

When he was done, Red scrambled his books into a pile and scraped back his chair.

Ellen looked up, frowning. "Where are you off to?"

"Workshop," said Red. He could hardly wait to finish that milking stool.

A teacherly glint snapped into Ellen's eyes. "Really, Red, d'you think you should? After your sorry exhibition in school today?"

"But—"

"What're you talking about?" Ma looked from Ellen to Red.

"Nothing," muttered Red.

"Nothing, my foot! He hardly knew any of his words. He was bottom of the class."

"I wasn't!" cried Red. "Not the bottom."

"Well, near enough. I never saw the like. You'd think you had no more brains than Chirpy Carmichael. If you'd put half as much effort into studying as you do fiddling about in that workshop, Red, you wouldn't do so badly in school. And what was that fight about at recess?"

"Fight?" said Ma. "Were you fighting, Red?"

Red shrugged.

"You know what your father and I tell you about fighting," said Ma, putting her hand on her waist. "What happened?"

Mac piped up. "He didn't start it, Ma. Eddie goaded him."

"Goaded!" Ellen snorted. "Sticks and stones. You're not a child, Red. You've got to control yourself. Now sit down and we'll go through those words again. I'm sorry, Ma. I'm not implying you didn't drill him right, but I won't have him make a fool out of himself again, like he did today. And out of me, too, for that matter."

"I've learned those words already. I'm not goin' over 'em again. You're not the boss of—"

"Red, she's your teacher, not just your sister," said Ma, pressing him down by the shoulder. "Mind what she says."

Seething, Red plunked down in his chair, nearly stepping on Clover's tail, who yowled and fled.

Ellen began to drill him.

Red fumbled and flustered through words he'd known perfectly well only minutes ago. The more he fumbled, the more sarcastic Ellen became. The only word Red figured he could spell right now, and with no difficulty whatsoever, was *crank*.

When at last Ellen let him go, it was near his bedtime. Bunch was already in bed, Mac had his nose stuck in a book, Pa was dozing by the fire and Ma was hooking her rug.

Burning inside, Red trudged up to the loft with a kerosene lamp. He thumped his books down on the chest at the bottom of his bed.

Something slipped to the floor.

It was that card. The one Aunt Lina had foisted on him.

Red put down the lamp and read through the card again.

The best sister in the world?

Cheerful? Soothing? Gentle?

His head throbbed, until he felt almost dizzy.

Red sat down by the chest and unscrewed his ink bottle. Ma wanted him to make the card personal, didn't she? She'd practically insisted that he change the words, hadn't she?

Red dipped his pen into the ink. He crossed out *wonderful*. He crossed it out several times until it was drowned in black ink. He crossed out *kind, thoughtful, sweet*. On he went, crossing out words until he got to the bottom. Then he began to write in new words, words he could spell perfectly well.

When he finished, Red sat back on his heels and read the card over.

The red mist of anger inside him began to clear.

He rubbed his inky fingers across his forehead. And then he remembered that the card was also supposed to be from Alex, Mac and Bunch.

He couldn't let them see it.

He couldn't let anyone see it, especially not Ma.

Or Ellen.

He thrust the card in the bottom of his chest under his clothes. Quickly, he changed into his pyjamas, blew out the lamp and got into bed.

Maybe he could still fix that card. Cross out the words he'd written and put in others.

What could he say about Ellen? She made good pies— the best lemon pies. And raisin pies. He could say that. She could tat lace like anything and darn socks so the mend hardly showed. She could be funny, too, when she took the notion, just like Ma. And the organ. She played well. She played in church sometimes, and often she'd bang out a tune on the pump organ in the parlour for a family singalong. Except she was always telling Red to pipe down, because he sang off key, and twisting his ear when he couldn't.

Red burrowed under the blankets and he pretended to be asleep when Mac came up.

• • •

Frost hit hard overnight. At breakfast the next day, Pa said they'd best get going pulling up the turnips. The sooner he sold them the better.

He hesitated, then asked Ellen, "D'you think maybe one of the boys could stay home after dinner to help? Would he miss much at school?"

Ellen nodded. "Of course, Pa. Mac can stay. I'll make sure he doesn't miss out. Red, now, he needs all the help he can get." She gave Red a look that made him wish that Pa and Ma didn't give a straw about education, like most of the families around them.

The rest of that week, Red and Mac helped Pa every spare moment. Mac stayed home a couple of afternoons, but Red had to go to school all day and help after. As long as it was light, they pulled turnips, their hands numb and red with cold. They cut off the roots, trimmed the tops and threw the turnips into the cart to bag later, or put down in the cellar, then gathered the greens for the cows. Each night, Red was exhausted. When he closed his eyes all he saw were turnip greens and red dirt.

Friday, they started to bag the turnips, and first thing

Saturday morning, when it was barely light, Red and Mac hurried out with Pa to finish. It was bitingly cold, and Red didn't look forward to a whole day of freezing hands, bagging turnips. Ma promised them a quick lunch for their midday meal because they'd be pressed for time.

"We'll have our main meal at suppertime, after you get the turnips off," said Ma. "And we'll celebrate Ellen's birthday then. I'll bake a nice big cake."

Ellen's birthday. Red had forgotten.

And that card! He'd never got around to changing it.

Good thing he'd hidden it. And that Ma had forgotten about it, too.

They worked hard all day. November days were short, and they had to make the most of the daylight hours. They put the best of the turnips into the bags, hands chilled and filthy, breath clouding in front of their faces, and sewed the bags closed. Red thought his arms would drop, but he kept going. Pa seemed worried, and in a hurry to get to the train station. The local farmers had spoken for a freight car to be dropped off at Applecross Station to take the turnips to town.

At last, all the turnips were bagged and ready to go. Mac and Pa hitched the horses to the heavy working wagon and began to drive the fifty-pound bags to the station.

Red stayed behind to do the chores. He was plain wiped, but he knew he had the easy part. He'd rather milk the cows, resting his head against their warm sides, and clean the stalls than be out in that biting wind, heaving bags of turnips onto the freight car.

The cows were drying up, so they didn't take long to milk. Red took the bucket of milk into the back porch to Ma, then fed the cows, filled the horses' mangers with hay, mucked out the stalls and stables and filled the water troughs in the barn. He'd just started to feed the pigs their vegetable peelings and slops at the far end of the barn when Pa and Mac returned. He heard Mac's voice coaxing the horses into the stable.

It was getting dark by the time Red was done. He pumped some water in the wellhouse and hurried to the back porch, eager to get out of that wind. As he scrubbed his hands at the basin in the porch, he glimpsed Pa at the kitchen table with Ma, Bunch and Mac.

He heard Pa say something in a low voice, followed by silence.

A strange, prickling silence.

Red wiped his hands and face on the threadbare towel and went into the kitchen.

In the gathering darkness, Pa sat still, his arms outstretched on the table, his shoulders sagging.

Red had never seen him look so tired. So defeated.

Ma's face was pinched and Mac looked . . . he looked concerned. Even Bunch was pale and staring.

"Pa?" said Red.

At last, Pa looked up. "The turnips. The price dropped. Dropped, like you wouldn't . . ." He let his breath out in a long hiss. "We owe more for the bags we put 'em in than we'll get for the turnips." Almost to himself, he murmured, "How in the world am I going to pay for that fertilizer?"

Red's chest squeezed tight. They'd owe money for the bags?

All that work, and they'd still *owe* money?

Ma twitched to her feet and struck a match to light the lamp.

"Never mind," she said, as the mantle flared into brightness. "We'll manage, somehow. We always do." Her chin jutted out sharply. "We've a lot to be thankful for— we've plenty to eat, and those caddies for credit at the store. We're far better off than most families 'round here. And as for those poor folks out west, what with the drought and everything, never mind those in the States . . ." Ma drew in a breath as though it pained her.

Pa lifted his head. "Oh, I guess we're rich, all right, compared to most." He slowly straightened his back. "And thank goodness, at least you children are getting an education. If you decide to farm it won't be because you've got no other option. You won't have to be at the mercy of weather and pests and markets." Pa thumped his fist on the table. "Jumpin' Jerusalem! You'll *have* some choices in life."

"That's right," said Ma, pacing up and down. "A lot of folks around here think we're plain foolish to have borrowed money to put Ellen through college, but they'll see. If each of you pays to put the next one through, there'll be no stopping you." She nodded emphatically. "And if Alex gets that scholarship, imagine! He'll have a degree!"

"But who do I pay for?" asked Bunch. "Ma?" She tugged Ma's apron. "Who do I pay for?"

"What, pet?" Ma's face unknotted as she looked down at Bunch. "Oh. Guess you don't pay for anyone. You get off free!"

Bunch's eyes brightened. "I get off free." She clapped her hands. "Free!"

Ma scooped her up. "No, you don't! Look at the dirt on you, Honey-Bunch! I'm going to have to scrub and scrub ..."

Bunch squealed.

Ma nodded at Red and Mac over the top of Bunch's head. "All right then, boys, snap to. We have a birthday to celebrate, and Alex is coming home. Go and get spruced up."

"Guess that means me, too." Pa pulled himself to his feet. "Where's Ellen, Kathleen?"

"Over at Myra's," said Ma. "I sent her there for the afternoon, so I could bake the cake. She's going to the station to meet Alex." In the distance, the train whistle shrilled. "There—they'll be here any minute."

"Red, did you get the milking done?" asked Pa.

"Yes, and cleaned out the barns, too."

Pa put his hand on Red's shoulder and squeezed.

"Oh, I must put out the old spoon with the fly to welcome Alex home," said Ma, her quick smile flashing. She gave Bunch a peck on the cheek. "Now let's get you cleaned up. Mercy, look at the child's face."

Red and Mac hurried upstairs to change their shirts and comb their hair. By the time they came down again, Ellen was back from the station with Alex.

Red rushed over to his older brother. He could've sworn Alex was taller. He looked so grown-up. His dark hair was brushed back, and in the new shirt that Ma had sewed for him, his shoulders seem wider. He almost looked like a town boy.

Everyone crowded around Alex, laughing and talking. And they laughed even more when they sat down to supper and Alex made a loud *ppphhhrrrrt*.

Ma had put out the whoopee cushion for him too, as an extra welcome.

Eagerly, Red tucked in to Ma's roast pork and gravy, with mashed potatoes, turnips and carrots. He almost forgot about the turnip crop, until he noticed how Ma seemed far away at times, and how Pa was a bit quiet, even for him.

But if Pa said they'd be all right, he knew they would be. Pa could turn his hand to anything; there was no one in Applecross, likely all of eastern Queens County, more resourceful than Pa. Any time there was a house to be fixed, a roof to be shingled or a barn to be built, Pa was the first one called. Not that he ever charged enough; Pa knew how hard it was for folks to get by. No one had much to barter with, let alone cold cash to pay. Pa often said he got paid in satisfaction, but when Cat-less Granny had heard that, she'd said you couldn't eat satisfaction.

When they finished with the roast, Ma cleared the dishes and headed to the pantry. "Now then, Ellen, you're not to get up," she said, with pretended severity. "You stay put."

"Well, whatever can be going on?" asked Ellen, trying not to smile.

Ma came back carrying the cake. It was smothered in rich cream frosting, and decorated with a smattering of candles. Under the plate were a couple of flat packages wrapped in brown paper.

Ma put the cake down in front of Ellen, and beside it the two packages.

Ellen smiled as everyone sang "Happy Birthday," but her smile seemed strained. She kept looking towards the back porch door.

After Ellen blew out the candles and cut the cake, Ma handed her the packages. "I know we normally don't do birthday presents, but it isn't every day you turn twenty-one."

Ellen glanced at the back porch again, then opened the presents. She made much of the crocheted lace from Ma and Pa, and the book Alex had brought her from Charlottetown. *Pride and Prejudice,* by Jane Austen. Red knew Ellen loved that book—she borrowed it enough from the library.

"Oh, I almost forgot." Ma reached into her apron pocket and handed Ellen a card. She squeezed Red's shoulder and whispered, "I found it in your chest and brought it down."

Red's heart jolted so hard he thought he'd die on the spot. His brain screamed at him to snatch away the card, but before he could reach across Mac and Alex to do it, Ellen had it in her hands.

She exclaimed at the picture of pansies and opened the card.

Her smile froze, then slowly faded.

"Thank you," she said at last. Her hand twitched.

Ma frowned. She reached for the card and put on her reading glasses.

Red wished the floor would open up wide and swallow him whole.

Ma went very still as she scanned the card. Then Pa read it.

Ma snapped the card down in front of Red, and gave him a glance as sharp as a rap on the head.

The card looked as if an angry spider had fallen into an ink bottle then crawled all over it.

Birthday Greetings to a Cranky Sister
Your many harsh and scolding ways
Your sharp and angry scowling face
Your smacking hands, your snapping words
Make you the most agggggravating sister in all the world.

"I don't mean any of it," gulped Red. "I meant to write something else. I meant to say . . . Ellen makes great pies. And plays the organ really well. I meant . . ."

Ma let her breath out in a long sigh. She looked weary to the bone.

Red licked his lips. "I also wanted to say that Ellen dresses neatly and . . . and she's a good teacher . . ."

Ellen burst into tears. She dashed into the hallway and ran upstairs.

Alex picked up the card. Then Mac. Red couldn't bear the grave look in Alex's brown eyes, or the disappointment in Pa's.

"I'm awfully sorry, Ma," said Red. "I was mad that day, and I forgot, with the turnips and everything."

"I don't know what you were thinking, Red!" said Ma. "There's no excuse for it."

Red knew that if Ma hadn't still been upset about the turnips she'd have given him a right good scolding. That she didn't just made it worse.

"Well," said Ma, tapping her hand down on the table, "I don't suppose it's just the card that upset her. I think . . ." Her eyes darted to the back door. "Likely she was hoping Stew would come by."

She hesitated, then went upstairs after Ellen.

Bunch picked up the card and tried to spell out the words, until Pa put it away. No one said anything more about it, but the fun of having Alex home for the night was lost in the disapproving silence.

• • •

Sunday morning, when Ellen came down to breakfast, she seemed back to her normal self. She smiled and joked and joined in the conversation.

Red couldn't. He knew he ought to say something to Ellen, but he didn't know where to start.

When he was ready for church, he headed outside to the verandah to wait for Mac and Alex. There was a keen wind gusting, for all it was sunny. Clover, who'd been scratching at the door, went streaking inside to escape the cold, but Red felt better standing out there. He gazed across the red furrows of the front field—Pa had the straightest furrows in all of Applecross—then at the empty turnip field to the side. Strips of red, clumpy soil, where they'd pulled the turnips, alternated with bands of weeds. It looked bleak and sorry.

The door behind him creaked open. It was Ellen.

"Red, I want to have a word."

Red paled. He knew he had it coming. "Ellen, I just want to—"

"No." Ellen put up her hand. "Let me talk first."

Red bowed his head and nodded.

Ellen took a deep breath. "I guess I've been hard on you, Red, and, well, I just want to say I'm sorry. I know I'm not the most patient sister." Her eyes almost gleamed with her old snap. "And I s'pose we both have a temper, but I will try to be more patient, all right?"

Red felt like he'd been punched. "I'm sorry, Ellen. I'm really . . . I didn't mean it. I was just—"

"It's all right. I know you didn't." Ellen twisted his ear, then straightened his collar. "Now try and get yourself to church in a decent state, will you?"

The boys set off across a succession of fields, lanes and wood trails, to the United Church in Sprucecliffe. Ma, Pa, Ellen and Bunch would come later, with Flash and the buggy.

On the way, Alex told Mac and Red that he'd talked it over with Ma and Pa and decided to apply for that scholarship to get his degree. He couldn't ask Ellen to pay for any more than his two years of college, so if he didn't get that scholarship he wouldn't go. But if he did get it, he'd work summers to pay Mac's way to college, so Mac wouldn't have to do an extra year in school waiting for Alex to finish. The talk then turned to Mrs. McDermott's boarding house in Charlottetown. She'd been a war bride from England and she cooked all manner of strange things, like Yorkshire pudding, which wasn't a pudding at all but something she served with a roast.

Normally, Red loved to hear Alex's stories of the big city, and his imitations of Mrs. McDermott's accent, but today he barely took it in. His thoughts wove around Ellen and her grumpiness, the card and the turnips, and the way Ma had looked all angry and determined when she'd talked about how they were each to pay for the others' education, sort of hand over hand.

He remembered the fence posts he'd helped Pa fix that summer. Pa had said each and every post had to be good and strong to support the whole fence.

Red walked on, barely noticing when the wood trail opened onto Lower Sprucecliffe Road, or the part he always watched out for, when the road turned and he caught his first glimpse of the wide blue waters of the Strait.

At church, Red tried to sit still and not fidget, but he couldn't. He looked across the aisle and down two pews at Stewart Gillis, who sat with his parents and his younger brother, Gavin.

Stewart had dark eyebrows, sunk-in eyes and a long, pointed nose. Girls were supposed to be crazy about him, just like they were crazy about Alex. Red couldn't figure out why. Alex was friendly and looked well enough, but Stewart had a dreadful temper. Even from here, Stew looked proud and . . . what was that word he'd learned in school the other day? Intimidating. That was it.

Red glanced at Ellen. She sat straight, her eyes fixed on Reverend Nicholls like her life depended on it. Her hands were tight in her lap.

Red wondered if that book *Pride and Prejudice* was about folks like Stew and Ellen.

After church, Ma and Pa lingered outside in the brisk sunshine to talk to the neighbours. Voices filled the air and, above them all, Ma's laughter rang out, generous and flowing. Red was glad she didn't laugh all stingy and jerky like Gooley's Ma.

Red scanned the crowds for Stewart. The front yard of the church, which sloped steeply down to the road, was bustling with folks. On the other side, a patchwork of gently rolling fields, stitched together by hedgerows, eased down to the wide blue sea. The water danced like diamonds, all sparkling and bright.

And Ellen, talking to a group of friends by the corner of the church, was also sparkling and bright—like she hadn't a care in the world.

Red finally spotted Stew's tall, lanky figure. He was alone, leaning on the fence at the side of the church, overlooking the old part of the cemetery. His face was about as sparkling as the mouldering headstones on which his eyes were fixed. Gavin stood nearby with Jim and Lewis, a couple of boys from Clearwater.

"Come on," said Mac. "We'd best get walking home—if we can tear Alex away from those girls." He grinned as he looked at the bright dresses and hats clustered around their brother.

"You go on ahead," said Red. "I'll come later."

Weaving through the crowds, Red worked his way over to Gavin. He had no idea what he could do, but he just knew he had to do *something*.

"How're ya doin', Gav?" He thumped Gavin's back and nodded to the other boys.

Gavin punched Red's arm. "Good. Real good. How's yourself?"

Red saw Stewart glance over his shoulder at him and frown.

Red licked his lips. A ragged idea began to form in his

head. "So . . . so what's your teacher like, in Clearwater?" he blurted.

"Miss MacDonald?" Gavin's face wrinkled in puzzlement. He looked at Jim and Lewis and shrugged. "All right, I guess. I mean she's . . . what d'you want to know for?"

"Ellen's teaching our school, you know." Red hooked his thumbs around his suspenders.

"Yeah, so what?"

"So, she's a really good teacher." Red raised his voice. "Smart. Real smart. She's the best teacher we've had in Applecross. She's teaching the pupils like you wouldn't believe, even the dumb ones. And pies. Can she bake pies. And play the organ. You've heard her. No one plays like her. She's some smart, I'm tellin' you."

Red saw Stewart half turn towards him. As though he was listening.

"What?" Gavin squinted at Red. "What're you on about?"

Red knew he sounded as crazy as the crows, but he ploughed on anyway. "She's a neat dresser, too. And . . . and accomplished, making lace. I guess she's the best teacher we've ever had. The trustees think awfully highly of her. They won't like it much when she gets married and leaves . . ." Red saw Stewart twitch and continued, louder, "I guess they'll be some upset. And the pupils, too. Of course, Ellen has a temper but she never really means

96

it. Sometimes she gets mad, but she usually gets over it fast. She's just—"

"Ha!" The confused look on Gavin's plump face cleared. A glint came into his eyes. "I bet Miss MacDonald is worse in the temper department than *your* sister. Miss MacDonald's got some mean mouth on her. And the strap. Oho! Can she ever swing it." He swiped his hand across his nose. "Does your sister strap?"

"No," said Red. "But she could. I guess."

Gavin let out a scoffing laugh. "I bet your sister can't strap half as good as Miss MacDonald. I bet she can't strap worth a bean. When Miss MacDonald gets riled, I'm telling ya, you'd better watch out." He looked at Jim and Lewis, who nodded eagerly and insisted that Miss MacDonald was the worst strapper in the district, likely all of Queens County—no, the fiercest teacher in Prince Edward Island, maybe even the entire Maritimes.

Red couldn't think of a single word to say back. Ellen didn't believe in the strap. Seemed like she was always letting him down.

He saw Stewart stride away down the road.

When at last Red managed to shake himself free, Stewart was nowhere in sight, and his own family had already left. Red sprinted up the road, his legs straining against the slope, then cut into the path through the woodlot. Bad enough he'd made a right fool of himself, he didn't want to be late for dinner, too. He raced down the trail, dodging branches.

As he neared the end of the trail, where it opened onto a furrowed field, someone sprang out from behind a clump of spruce and grabbed him by his jacket collar.

"Gotcha!" It was Stewart Gillis. He had a spark in his eye that looked as if it was liable to burst into flames any minute.

Red tried to wrench free but Stewart's grip tightened.

"Oh, no you don't. I want a word with you, lad." He shook Red. "Now. What was that you said about Ellen getting married? Is she seeing anyone else?"

"What? No. Let me go."

"Then what the heck were you talking about back there?"

"Nothing. I was just trying to . . . trying to help. Make peace between you."

Stewart's face darkened like thunder. "Who asked you? Ellen didn't, I bet."

"'Course she didn't. She'd kill me if she knew."

"Oh, she won't have to. I'll do it first." Stew's nostrils pinched together. "All right, then. Who put you up to it? Someone around here, trying to make mischief? Is that it? Some man, trying to cut in? Rub my nose in it?"

"No! I told you, I was just trying to help. Look, Ellen's got a temper, but if she says she never wants to see you again, she doesn't really mean it. You know what she's like. She's—"

Red staggered as Stewart abruptly let go.

"I know what she's like, all right." Stewart's mouth was a thin line. "Your sister has far too much a mind of her own. She's been putting me off long enough. All that talk about keeping on teaching. I told her she could just forget the whole thing if she—"

"Hold on, now!" cried Red. "She's not putting you off. She promised Pa and Ma she'd pay for Alex to get through college, and—"

"I know that! I'm not faulting her for minding your parents. Education is a fine thing and I'm all for it, except now she says she might want to keep teaching after we're married! I don't want my wife working like I can't support her. She's always spouting off about—"

"But that's Ellen," cried Red. "She's . . . she's opinionated. She's got opinions about near everything."

Stewart let his breath out in disgust. "She's got more opinions than a porcupine's got quills. Going on about women's education . . ."

"She's always at me, too," cried Red. "Telling me I spend too much time in the workshop, like it's any of her business . . ."

" . . . about the state of the country, and how women could run things better . . ."

"... and that I should learn more poetry by heart, like Mac ..."

"... and how women ought to be able to preach, and get paid the same for teaching as men ..."

"... and even after Ma's drilled my spelling, she's got to drill me all over again—*oww!*"

Stewart had grabbed Red's ear.

"What did you say?" cried Stew.

"Let go!"

"You ingrate! You snivelling ingrate! Are you blaming your sister for helping you?"

"Oww! Let go!"

"D'you think it's easy for her? D'you think Ellen wants to spend extra time drilling you? She works hard, Ellen. There's no better teacher on the Island. How dare you go sassing her!" Stewart twisted Red's ear, then let go.

"But—"

"Get out of here," growled Stewart. "Go on, before I give you a good tanning."

Red turned and ran. He ran so fast he thought his lungs would burst. He raced through fields and trails, stumbling and tripping over roots, but he didn't let up until he reached home. Outside the back door, he bent over double, gasping.

When at last he went inside, Ma was taking the roast out of the oven. "Where in the world did you get to? It's not like you to be late for dinner." She put the roast on the table and tapped his back. "Go on, wash up. Yes, I know, you've only been to church, but wash anyway."

Red's heart had nearly settled down to normal by the time they sat down to eat. He dug into his roast beef and mashed potatoes. They tasted some good. He finished his carrots and turnips. Then he had another helping of roast beef and potatoes, slipping Tubbs, who sat below the table, a small piece of beef. By the time he started on his raisin pie, he'd decided it was a real good thing he hadn't talked Stew into making up with Ellen.

Stew was clearly a few bales short of a load.

They'd just finished eating when they heard a horse coming up the lane.

Ma went over to the front sitting room window. "Why it's . . ." She turned to look at Ellen. "It's Stewart."

Red's stomach began to somersault. He wished he hadn't had that third sliver of pie.

"It's nothing to me," said Ellen, flushing. She sat still while Stewart knocked on the front door, like someone who'd never been to the house before.

Pa tried to hide his smile as Ma went to open the door.

"Ellen," called Ma. "Stewart wants to talk to you."

"You can tell Mr. Gillis that I'm not at home," said Ellen, loudly.

Red shifted uneasily. If Stewart was there on account

of anything he'd said, and Ellen wouldn't even talk to him, Red could be in big trouble.

He cleared his throat. "Ellen. Maybe you'd better—"

"Who asked you?" snapped Ellen.

Ma came back to the kitchen. Her face was solemn but laughter leapt in her eyes. "Now, Ellen. I don't think he's going 'til—"

"Ellen!" yelled Stew from the door.

"Go away!" she shouted.

There was silence. Ellen's face turned pale. She looked at Ma.

Ma gave a quick, sharp nod.

Ellen sprang to her feet, then froze as a strange wailing filled the air.

"Ell-llen, Ell-llen, give me your answer do! I'm half crazy, all for the love of you . . ."

It was the worst singing Red had ever heard. Worse than cats spitting and fighting. Jumpin' Jerusalem, Red could sing like a canary compared to old Stew.

Ma's laughter pealed out and they all began to laugh. Except for Ellen.

She rushed to the door. "Stewart Gillis, don't you dare . . ."

Red, Mac and Alex sprinted across to the front window.

Red saw Stewart, half laughing, half singing, grab hold of Ellen's hands and pull her down the verandah steps towards him. Ellen was laughing and crying as she let him hug her, then hugged him back.

"Come away, boys," said Ma, trying to keep a straight face. "No staring, now."

Red turned away from the window.

He felt an awful lot like that time when he'd been seven, and he'd gone on a ride at the Exhibition in Charlottetown, during Old Home Week. When he'd got off, his brains had felt all addled.

• • •

The dishes were washed and put away before Ellen came back inside with Stewart. There was the faintest trace of pink around her eyes, but she was smiling. She and Stew were holding hands.

Ellen slitted her eyes at Red and came up close. "Stew told me what you did." She twisted his ear. "Don't. You. Ever. Do. That. Again." She bent down to kiss his cheek.

Stewart twisted Red's other ear—harder than Ellen—then thumped his back. "Ah, but you're a good lad."

Ma put her head around the pantry door and called out, "Stewart, would you like some raisin pie? Ellen made it, and you know her pies."

Stew lifted Ellen's hand and kissed it. "I certainly do. She's a dab hand at pies, my Ellen."

Then all the grown-ups—Alex with them—sat down at the table, laughing and talking like nothing had ever happened.

Red opened the porch door and went outside, followed by Mac.

"What did Ellen mean, don't do it again?" asked Mac.

Red shrugged. "I guess I went and talked to Stew."

"You went and talked to *Stew*?" Mac's mouth fell open. "What did you say to bring him 'round?"

Red stood still for a moment. He jiggled his head like he was shaking water out of his ears. "I don't . . . I don't rightly know."

The only thing he did know was that if Ellen and Stew ever fought again, he was not getting caught in the middle.

He sure as heck didn't need the aggravation.

UPSIDE DOWN AND
RIGHT SIDE UP

A MEAN NOVEMBER WIND KNIFED THROUGH the air as Red and Mac jogged home from school for dinner at noon. The sky was bleak with lowering clouds, and the bare fields on either side of the road looked cold and shivery. Ellen hurried along behind them, pulling on Bunch's hand.

Red put on a spurt as he ran up their lane. He saw the big circular saw set up near the woodshed out back, with piles of fresh sawdust around it. Pa had decided to cut some extra firewood—over and above the cords he'd already cut that summer—because the almanac predicted a bad winter.

Red burst in through the back porch door, just ahead of Mac. Clover, who was curled up by the stove in the kitchen, twitched against the gust of cold air. Red flung off his jacket and shoes and hurried into the warmth of the kitchen. His mouth watered at the smell of the ham and potatoes Ma was taking out of the oven.

Pa was already at the table with Tinker MacPhee. Tinker's grey hair and whiskers were scraggly, as usual, and his cheeks crossed over with fine red veins. There was a faint trace of sawdust on his baggy pants, as well as on the many layers of flannel shirts he always wore.

"How's it goin', boys?" asked Tinker, his watery blue eyes crinkling. "Brains growin' good?"

Red grinned. "Growin' real good," he said, glancing at Ma.

Ma shook her head. She was a great one for picking him up on grammar, but Red knew she wouldn't embarrass Tinker for the world. He lived in a shack over in Clearwater, and did any odd jobs he could get. Ma always said Pa gave Tinker more wood than he'd earned for his work, but then, she always fed him well and loaded him up with baking or bags of potatoes, insisting they'd go to waste if he didn't take them home. And every fall when they killed a pig or cow, she was sure to give him a roast, or some chops.

Ellen and Bunch came in at last, along with a bitter jab of cold air. Ma put the carrots and mashed turnips on the table, along with the relish.

Red dug into his potatoes—no one made scalloped

potatoes like Ma—and remembered to chew with his mouth closed when Ma raised her eyebrow at him and touched her lips.

Tinker wasn't any too particular with his manners, Red noticed, but when you were grown-up you didn't have to be. Tinker balanced bits of carrots on his knife and never dropped one. Red would have liked to try that—it was some trick—but he knew he'd catch it from Ma later if he did.

Pa finished his apple crumble, then gulped down the last of his tea. "Best get going, Tink. That firewood isn't obliging enough to cut itself."

Red knew Pa was in a hurry to get it done, so that as soon as it snowed he could take Flash and the sleigh into the back woods to cut some fine hardwood. He'd take that to the mill to be sawed into boards for the tobacco caddy orders they got from Morrison's store, over in Clearwater. They already had their first order of the winter, and were partway through it.

Tinker groaned as he got to his feet. "Trees these days. Now, when I was a lad, 'round Mac and Red's age, I mind how the trees fell down and sawed themselves into tidy two-foot lengths. Split themselves, too. Yah!" He sucked in his breath. "Them were the days."

"Why, I don't recollect any such feats, Tinker," said Pa. "Your memory's goin' on ya, Dunc, that's what it is."

"Hear that, boys?" said Pa. "Best stay in school so your memory remains sharp, like Tinker's."

Ma glanced at the boys, then solemnly pushed over the package of trick gum. "Here now, have a stick of gum to take with you, Tinker."

"Don't mind if I do," he said.

As soon as he went to pull out a piece, a spring snapped over on his finger.

"Oww!" Tinker started back.

Everyone burst out laughing.

"Should'a known you were up to somethin', Kathleen," hooted Tinker. "That's some gadget you got there."

"It comes from the same trees you were talking about, Tinker," said Ma, her face all innocent. "The gum obligingly packs itself for a chew, but it's a mite particular about who picks it."

Tinker roared with laughter.

"Come on, boys, back to school," said Ellen, getting to her feet.

Red and Mac bundled themselves into their coats. Red put on his cap, pulling the flaps down over his ears, and picked up one of Ma's cinnamon rolls to see him to school. They jogged down the road, chuckling at Ma's trick. Ma was always so clever and quick.

But as they crunched through the dried leaves up to the school door, Red sobered.

Poetry recitation. His class had poetry recitation that afternoon.

Why couldn't it have been Mac's class? Mac liked reciting. He could be an awful show-off, spouting poetry like there was no tomorrow. He even knew all of Thomas Gray's "Elegy Written in a Country Churchyard" by heart.

Red hung up his cap and coat and took a long drink of water from the bucket in the porch. Samuel Johnson, a tall, serious boy in Grade Ten, had the job of school janitor for the year; he filled the bucket each morning from the farm across the road. Ellen said Sam was the most reliable janitor they'd had; he even kept the school clean to her satisfaction.

In the schoolroom, Sam was feeding wood into the stove, *thunk, clunk, thunk, clunk.* Thank goodness Ellen allowed it to be lit now—it was easier to think when the school wasn't as cold as a barn.

"*When I consider how my light is spent,*" murmured Red, as he warmed his hands by the stove. He'd better remember to say *spent*, not *bent*. *Bent* came in a few lines down. He'd only picked Milton's poem "On His Blindness" because it was the shortest he could find. Ellen complained that he raced through his recitations with no expression whatsoever, but Red figured getting through it mattered more than any highfalutin expression.

As Ellen came in with Bunch, Gooley and a few other tardy pupils rushed through the door after her. Ellen gave them a sharp look and told them to take off their caps. She assigned the other children their exercises and reading passages, then called up Red's class for the poetry recitation.

Red shuffled to the end of the line, trying to keep the words in his head, and in the right order. He glanced at Shona Murray, who was reading her history book, her fingers twirling the end of her braid.

Seemed like she didn't even know he was alive.

Not that he wanted her to notice, if he flubbed his lines and made a right fool of himself.

Red barely heard the other pupils reciting. Peter went first, then Gooley, Archie and Fiona.

"When I consider how my light is bent," muttered Red. No, wait. Was it *bent* or *spent*?

Fiona was up, reciting with great expression, when the school door slammed open.

Tommy Munn rushed in.

"Tommy," snapped Ellen. "What is the meaning—?"

"Ellen!" Tommy was panting so hard, Red thought his thin body would snap in two. "Your Ma. Wants. All o' yez. Home. Your Pa's. Hurt."

The word *hurt* came out high and sharp.

Red stood frozen, staring at Tommy.

"What happened?" cried Ellen.

"Yez got to hurry!" gasped Tommy. "He's hurt real bad." He dashed outside and ran off.

Ellen's face went white. "Children," she said, her voice strangely calm. "Please gather your things. School is dismissed. Samuel, close the damper on the stove and lock up after the children have left. Red, Mac, Bunch, come. Put on your coats."

Red shoved on his coat without bothering to button it up, grabbed his cap and rushed outside with Mac. They bounded across the yard and down the road after Tommy, with Ellen running behind, tugging on Bunch's hand.

Red thought his chest would explode by the time he reached home. Tommy Munn, bent over gasping, was by the back porch door with his older brother, Henry. Henry tried to hold Red back, but Red pushed through the door and into the kitchen, followed by Mac.

In a series of flashes Red saw Ma crying, hand against her mouth. Maisie Munn with her arm around Ma. Pa slumped at the table with Tinker, Callum MacMillan and Joshua Munn hovering around him.

Oh, thank the Lord, Pa wasn't . . .

But Pa's head was down, and his face ashen.

It took Red a few seconds to register.

Pa's hand.

His left hand, wound in a white towel.

No, not white. That colour—staining through.

Then Ellen burst in, along with Bunch.

"Ma! What's happened?" cried Ellen.

"Hold that firm now, Duncan," said Callum. "The doctor'll be here any minute."

Ellen had her arms around Ma, who was gasping, " . . . accident. His fingers . . ."

"Pa?" said Red.

"I'm all right," whispered Pa, looking up. But his face was grey.

Red heard the door open behind him. It was Dr. MacLeod.

"All right now, let's see what's goin' on. Move over a bit, Joshua. What happened?"

Tinker looked like he was about to cry. "My fault. I was in a rush, darn it—pardon me, ladies—and I pushed that trunk too fast. Oh God, Duncan, I'm so sorry."

As though from a great distance, Red saw the doctor lift Pa's hand and unwind the towel. He drew in a sharp breath, and wrapped it over again.

Red's stomach pitched.

A hand should have fingers, shouldn't it?

He heard Ma cry out and Ellen gasp. Bunch was sobbing, and Mac was as pale as a ghost.

Dr. MacLeod's calm presence seemed to hold the room together.

"All right, Duncan," said the doctor. "I've got the car right here."

Red hadn't even heard it come up the lane.

"Keep the pressure on, Duncan. I'll take you in to Charlottetown, to the hospital. We'll get you fixed up in no time."

"I'll get your things, Ma," said Ellen.

"No." Ma shook her head. "I can't go. Who'll mind Bunch? And . . . oh, I can't think."

Red had never seen Ma like that. He felt as if the ground had collapsed under his feet.

"Don't you fret, Kathleen," said Mrs. Munn. "We'll be here to help."

"That's right," said Joshua Munn. "You git along, now."

"Alex," said Ma, pressing her hands to the sides of her face. "How do I get word to Alex?"

"We'll call him, Kathleen, and let him know, so he can meet you at the hospital," said Mrs. Munn.

"Ma, d'you want me to come with you?" asked Ellen.

"No, you must stay, Ellen. Take care of the others."

"We can manage," croaked Red. "Take Ellen if you need her."

"We'll mind everything," said Mac.

"No." Ma wiped her face. "I want you to stay here, Ellen."

Red felt a burst of relief that Ellen would be there to hold things straight.

Ma scrambled into her coat and hat. She pulled Red, Mac, Bunch and Ellen into a quivering hug, then hurried after Pa and Dr. MacLeod.

Pa got into the car, cradling his left hand like a baby swaddled in a rusty red cloth. He looked like an old man.

The car drove off fast—the fastest Red had ever seen it go—and disappeared down the road.

Red stood there, staring after it, unable to move.

"Come on, let's go inside," said Ellen. "We'll get a nice hot cup of tea going." She picked up Bunch, who was crying, and kissed her cheek.

Red followed Ellen into the kitchen.

Maisie Munn was at the table, scrubbing that dull red stain.

Red rushed outside and vomited right over Ma's frostbitten pansies.

Henry Munn, who was big and beefy, thumped Red's back. "There now, don't you go frettin'. Doc MacLeod'll take care of everythin'. He's the best doctor on the whole darn Island."

"That he is," squeaked Tommy.

Red wiped his mouth and straightened up.

It was all part of the wrongness of this day, to see Tommy look so stricken and sympathetic, instead of making snide comments about big fellas like Mac and Red sittin' around school to avoid honest work.

Ellen came outside and put her arm around Red. "It's going to be all right. Everything's going to be all right."

"But Pa. What if he . . . ?" Red's face crumpled.

Ellen gripped him by the shoulders. "Now you listen to me, Roderick MacRae. Pa has had an accident. That is all. He is going to be just fine, d'you hear me?" Her mouth trembled slightly, but her eyes blazed, defying him to say different.

Somehow, the conviction in Ellen's voice slowed the pitching in his stomach.

Red didn't know how he got through that afternoon. Everything seemed upside down. Even the cats sensed something was wrong; Tubbs fled to the barn, while Clover tried to wind around Bunch's legs, as though to comfort her. It was Ellen who kept things from falling clean apart. She talked to the steady stream of visitors who dropped by—some curious, some concerned. She thanked them for the food they brought, got Bunch rolling cookie dough, and kept up a whirl of activity, baking, cooking and cleaning.

Later, she made up a sign and gave it to Red. "Go and tack that on the school door, will you?"

Red stared at the sheet of paper: *School closed until further notice.*

With a handful of tacks from the workshop, Red dragged himself down the road. He couldn't jog as he normally did. He trudged across the empty schoolyard, wading through leaves the colour of dried blood.

It felt strange being there. The schoolhouse was so quiet and deserted. The silence seemed to batter his ears.

Just a few hours ago he'd been inside the schoolroom, dreading his recitation. Right now, he'd give anything to be back in there, even with the humiliation of messing up his lines and having everyone laugh.

He'd barely got home when Mrs. Lowry arrived. She was tall and thin, with a long, bony face and small, eager eyes. Red didn't much like her. He knew Ma didn't care for her either, because she was always spreading gossip.

"I'm sorry for your troubles," she said. Her eyes darted about as she handed Ellen a plateful of ginger cookies.

"It's not troubles," cried Red. "Pa's not dead! He's just—"

"Red, hush." Ellen's smile was bright and hard as she turned to their visitor. "Thank you, Mrs. Lowry. I dare say the stories you've heard are highly exaggerated, but rest assured, Pa's just had a slight accident to his hand. He will be home soon, and in fine kilter."

"Well, I'm happy to hear it, I'm sure," said Mrs. Lowry, looking offended.

As the afternoon wore on and the sun dipped lower in

the sky, Ellen said, "Go on, boys. Chores have to be done. We must carry on as usual."

It was good to have something to do. They milked the cows—they were near dry—and carried the milk to the porch. Silently, they went back to the barn to feed and water the animals and muck out the stalls. Mac didn't whistle at all. When they finished, they both headed to the henhouse behind the big barn to feed and water the hens. Usually, Ma did that.

Ellen had supper on when they got back inside. Leftover ham and scalloped potatoes.

Red blinked. Was it only earlier that day they'd eaten it together, laughing and talking? He could hardly bear to look at it, never mind eat it.

"When will we hear from Ma?" he asked.

"Sometime this evening, I expect." Ellen put the bread on the table. "Likely she'll call the Munns, when she gets a minute."

A few years back, Mr. Munn had paid to have a phone line put in to his house. Pa had decided against it because it was too dear—he'd still been paying for Ellen's education then. Red had never hankered for the phone; Gooley said one of his sisters spent half her time listening in on every call that came through the party line. But today, it would have been a relief to have had one.

After supper, Ellen insisted that they go over their lessons. "We've got to carry on with the normal routine, even if there's no school tomorrow. I don't want you boys getting behind."

Red tried to remember the normal routine. It took some effort. He'd study and then . . . then he and Mac would go with Pa to the workshop in the little barn to make the tobacco caddies.

The tobacco caddies.

They hadn't completed that last order for two hundred.

Mr. Morrison gave all his orders to Pa because no one else made the caddies as well. Pa always sized them just right—six by six by five inches—and made sure that the edges lined up true. Then he planed the sides smooth and trimmed the bottom with mitred moulding. The lids that he provided, to be put on after the caddies were filled, always fit just right, as well as the mouldings to go around the top.

Making those caddies was their only way to get credit at the store. When each order was complete, Pa took the caddies, along with their tops and upper mouldings, to put in the freight car for Hickey and Nicholson's over in Charlottetown. He got the shipping bill from the station agent and took it to Morrison's to show he'd filled the order. Mr. Morrison then gave him credit for it at the store, and meanwhile, Hickey and Nicholson's filled the caddies with five-inch plugs of chewing tobacco and gave the store a discount for supplying the boxes.

Ma often said she didn't know how they'd manage without that credit.

But how in tarnation would they finish those caddies without Pa?

It was just about Red and Mac's bedtime when Mrs. Munn came running over. She said that Ma had telephoned from the hospital to let them know she was staying the night, and that Alex was with her.

"How's Pa?" asked Ellen.

Red was glad she'd asked; he couldn't have.

Mrs. Munn caught Ellen's warning glance and her cheeks bulged upwards into a painfully insincere smile. "He's doing real well, I guess. As well as well can be. Don't you worry none about it." The hair on her upper lip twitched like nervous antennae sniffing fear.

"All right, boys," said Ellen crisply. "Off to bed now."

Up in the loft, Red and Mac quietly got into bed. Red tossed and turned. He could hear Mac, too, turning and sighing.

"Mac," whispered Red. "You asleep?"

"No."

"Mac, what're we going to do?"

Mac's voice trickled over, thin and lost. "I don't know."

Red stared up into the darkness. If Mac was concerned,

it had to be bad. Really bad. He pressed his face against the pillow. He was too old to cry, but his eyes leaked.

● ● ●

When he woke the next morning, Red knew right away Pa wasn't there.

The house didn't sound right. Pa was always the first one up; he got the stove going and put on the porridge.

Red could hear the clunk of the stove opening, the thud of wood being thrown in and the thunk of the pot on the stove. But none of it sounded like Pa; it sounded Ellen-ish. Sharp and quick, instead of solid and steady, like Pa.

It was a relief to get up and start on the chores, to be busy with something. He and Mac worked in silence; they milked and fed the cows—grinding some turnips for their feed—mucked out the stalls, then fed the horses and cleaned the stables. They watered the livestock, fed the pigs and even cleaned out the pigsty, though it didn't really need it yet. Then they went to the henhouse to feed and water the hens and look for eggs—there weren't many this time of year, with the days so short.

More visitors came by, and later, Dr. MacLeod dropped in to bring them news and pick up some clothes to take back for Pa and Ma.

"Your Pa's going to be in the hospital a little longer, but your Ma said she'll try and get home on the train soon."

Red wanted to ask about Pa's hand, but the words stuck like a burr in his throat.

Then Ellen asked, "And how is Pa's hand?"

Dr. MacLeod looked at them with his keen brown eyes. He wasn't one to mince words, Ma always said. Right now Red wasn't sure if he was more glad of it or sorry.

"Well now, he's lost three fingers just above the second knuckle." Dr. MacLeod indicated the last three fingers of his left hand. "That's the bad news. But the good news is he's still got his thumb and forefinger and that's a real blessing. I believe that, after a while, he'll be able to do just about everything he's always done. Don't worry, he's going to be just fine."

"Pa doesn't have fingers?" Bunch's eyes filled and her face wobbled.

Ellen picked her up and cuddled her.

Red hardly noticed Dr. MacLeod leave.

Three fingers.

Three fingers gone. How in the world would Pa manage everyday chores, never mind the delicate work of making those caddies?

Red went outside to the bleak November sunshine.

It seemed an insult to have the sun shining.

He paced along the hard ground from the house to the big barn. Tubbs, who was perched on the wellhouse roof, watched him with solemn golden eyes.

Mr. Munn came by a short while later with Tinker. Red heard him tell Ellen not to go frettin'—he'd help Tinker saw the rest of the firewood. And once the snow was down, he said, he'd help Pa cut hardwood to take to the mill.

Hardwood. To cut into boards for the caddies.

Except they wouldn't need any more boards if they couldn't make the caddy order.

A few years back, Simon MacPhee, from Marram Point, had also made tobacco caddies. But Mr. Morrison had stopped giving him orders because, he said, no one made the caddies as fine as Duncan MacRae and his boys.

Red heard the big circular saw start up in the backyard as Tinker and Mr. Munn began to cut the tree trunks into two-foot lengths for firewood.

Red stared at the worn wooden door of the workshop, at the near end of the little barn. For a moment he felt as if all the air had been squeezed out of his chest.

Then he went into the kitchen. "Mac. Coming to the workshop?"

Ellen's head snapped up. "I don't want you fellas in there. Not without—" She bit her lip.

"We've got an order for two hundred caddies." Red's

mouth was dry. "I guess we'd better get on with it."

He saw the hesitation on Ellen's face. The anxiety.

"We've been working on those caddies for years now," said Red. "I've been helpin' out ever since I was five. Pa's taught us every stage of it, and he's shown us how to be careful with those tools."

He looked at Mac for support.

Mac's face was uneasy. He'd never been as comfortable with the tools as Red. He'd just as soon have had his nose in a book.

But Mac nodded. "Red knows as much as Pa does about making those caddies."

"All right," said Ellen, at last. "But be . . ." She slid right over what she was about to say, and finished with, " . . . be on time for dinner."

Red nodded. He and Mac headed outside and across the yard to the workshop.

It didn't feel right being in there without Pa. There was the familiar smell of sawdust but the workshop was cold and damp—Pa always lit the stove before they got started. The tools were lined up tidily on the bench as usual; Pa kept things in good order.

Silently, the two boys got a fire lit in the stove. It crackled and hissed nervously as the flames worried about, then gathered strength.

Mac shut the stove door, then looked uncertainly at

Red. It was strange having Mac waiting for him to take the lead.

Red licked his lips. Pa always said the way to build anything was slow and easy, one step at a time.

"All right," he said. "Pa's already got some sides cut. I'll nail them together and you plane them, like you always do. I'll cut the moulding and nail it on. And then I'll cut some more sides for the rest of the order."

Mac nodded.

They set to work. The stack of finished boxes began to grow steadily. Red looked over Mac's work and a few times told him to plane the wood over. Mac sighed, and one time scowled, but he did it. Red knew that Mac understood the caddies had to be just as good as when Pa was around.

The pile of cut sides was getting lower. It had always been Pa's job to cut them, but they'd have to do it now, if they were to make the order.

Red looked at the crosscut saw, the sharp teeth. Pa had rigged up a one-cylinder gas engine to power the saw. It was some forceful. Pa always said you had to respect the tools, treat them with care.

Red picked up an oak board. The grain was fine and true. Despite the knot in his stomach, he felt some of his familiar pleasure at handling a fine piece of wood.

He could do it, he told himself.

He had to.

He'd made that milking stool without even thinking about it and cut all the pieces himself.

Carefully, Red marked out the right lengths on the board. He checked the markings twice. Then he powered up the saw. The engine came to life, purring true.

Red sat down, trying to keep his hands steady. He made sure his fingers were good and far from the edge of the saw.

He began to cut.

He felt Mac holding his breath and tried to make his own back less tight. Wetting his lips, Red began to whistle, pretending Pa's deep voice was guiding him, step by step.

Red didn't know how long he'd been cutting before he became aware of his stiff neck and aching shoulders. He straightened up and saw Ellen standing just inside the door, her arms wrapped around herself like she was holding her breath, too. He'd never even heard her enter.

Red stopped the engine.

"Come on in for dinner," said Ellen. Her eyes swept across the piles of cut wood, to the finished boxes. She patted Red's shoulder as he went by, then tweaked his ear.

After dinner, Red went straight back to the workshop. He examined the boxes they'd assembled, then sat down to cut some more sides. Mac didn't look entirely thrilled to be there, but he said nothing and kept planing.

They worked as long as the light lasted.

The next day, after the morning chores, Red hurried into the workshop again, while Mac studied, even though it was a Saturday. But after dinner, Mac came to help.

Red kept count of the finished boxes. When they got to two hundred, he made two more. He put one aside that Pa had made, along with one of his own, which he marked inside with a faint *R*. He glanced outside at the late-afternoon sunshine.

If he hurried, he could make it.

"I'll take these over to the station now, to load into the freight car," he said. "Then I'm going to Morrison's store with the shipping bill. Think you can manage the chores on your own?"

Mac's eyebrows snapped together. "Look, Red, I'm not faulting you for knowing more than me about makin' the caddies, but there's no call for you to act so bossy. Why the blazes d'you have to go to Morrison's today?"

Red's mouth set stubbornly. "Because I want Mr. Morrison to know we can do it." He barely refrained from adding, *dummy*.

Mac looked startled, then said, "I'll help you hitch up Flash."

Red nodded. He'd rather not handle Flash alone. Flash was most liable to run away when he was being hitched.

Together, Red and Mac packed the caddies into a couple of crates and carried them outside. It was brisk and

bright, with a clear blue sky. Red put the two extra caddies in an old sack on top of the crates. He went into the
house, washed and went upstairs to change into his good
pants. Pa always said when a man did business it was just
as well to be attired right.

"I'm taking the caddies to the station," he told Ellen.
"And I'm going to Morrison's with the shipping bill right
after. Need anything there?"

An approving gleam came into Ellen's eyes. "I believe
we need some baking powder, Red. Ma was saying it's getting low." She reached out to twist his ear, then patted his
shoulder instead.

Outside, Mac was waiting with Flash already harnessed to the light driving wagon. He helped Red load
the crates filled with the caddies, along with their tops
and mouldings.

"You'd better behave, Flash," said Mac, looking him
in the eye. "Just be firm with him, Red. Show him who's
boss."

Red climbed onto the seat and took the reins, trying to keep his hands steady. He'd driven Jean and the
working wagon lots of times, but he'd never driven
Flash by himself, not with the buggy or the light wagon.
Old Flash could be awfully persnickety when he took
the notion. Pa always said he had a bit of the racing
blood in him.

Red twitched the reins and Flash trotted off down the lane, turning the corner onto the road with just enough speed to show who was in charge.

It wasn't far to the station. Just down the road, past the Munn farm, then over the bridge, to the crossroads. Red pulled hard to turn Flash into the station lane on the other side of the bridge. Relief flooded him when Flash came to a stop.

The freight car was sitting on the siding. Red called out to Charlie Payne, the station agent, who asked after Pa, then helped him load the order. When they were done, Charlie made out the shipping bill from Morrison's store to Hickey and Nicholson's, and gave Red his copy.

Red folded it carefully over and across, creasing it nice and crisp, like Pa always did, then put it in his pocket. He climbed back onto the wagon seat, took a deep breath and snapped the reins. It was a struggle to get Flash to turn left onto Berryfield Road instead of back towards home, but Red managed it.

They rattled up and down the crests and dips of the winding red road, past an assortment of farmhouses, most neat and spruce, but a few rundown. One farm was so poor a grasshopper would have starved to death crossing it. Red turned Flash onto the road leading to Clearwater, then let him have his head. He told himself he could slow Flash down if he wanted to, except he was in a hurry to get to Morrison's.

Ma always said this part of the road was one of the prettiest on the Island. On the right, a patchwork of rolling fields sloped down to red cliffs and strips of sand, skirting the glistening blue sea. But Red kept his eyes fixed on Flash's tail and ears, and his hands at the ready to pull.

At last they reached Clearwater. When they neared the store, Red yanked on the reins so hard he practically stood. "Whoa. Stop now, Flash. Stop." Lucky for him, Flash was amenable to stopping, although he nickered, then lifted his tail and dumped a load, to show his disdain.

Red jumped down and tied Flash securely to the post. His hands were trembling. With the shipping bill and the two extra caddies under his arm, Red climbed up the front porch steps.

An old man with rheumy eyes and straggly grey whiskers glared at Red and nodded.

Inside the store, the usual group of men sat around the stove, most of them chewing tobacco. Mr. Morrison always said you'd never know times were so hard, the way tobacco flew off the shelves.

When the men saw Red, their chatter faded.

Red put the shipping bill down on the counter along with the caddies.

Kevin MacDonald, one of the men around the stove,

stopped mid-chew to ask, "How's your Pa doin', Red?"

Mr. Morrison hurried over from the back of the store. He was a short man with a deeply lined face and one thick eyebrow, like a furry caterpillar, right across his forehead. "What in the world you doin' here, Red? How's your Pa?"

"Evening, Mr. Morrison." Red took off his cap and nodded at the men around the stove. "Pa's doing fine. He'll be home any day now. Just wanted to bring in this shipping bill. We got those caddies done and loaded on the freight car." He cleared his throat. "Any new orders in?"

Mr. Morrison's forehead creased. He rubbed his hand across the top of his caterpillar brow, making it go all bristly. "Well, now. So your Pa had already filled the order, is that it?"

Red shook his head. "No, Mr. Morrison. Pa, Mac and I made about half together, but Mac and I finished the rest." Red saw the wary look on Mr. Morrison's face and pushed the two tobacco caddies over. "Go ahead. Take a look. One was made by Pa, and one by Mac and me. You won't spot the difference."

Mr. Morrison shot Red a piercing glance, then began to examine the caddies. He turned one around, then the other. "Well, darned if I can tell. Which is which?"

"I marked *R* inside one," said Red, pointing to the faint pencil mark he'd made.

Mr. Morrison looked them over again, then smiled broadly. "You tell your Pa, the orders will come to him like usual. Always said, no one makes 'em as good as you MacRaes."

"That's for sure," said Kevin MacDonald. He grinned, showing his black-stained teeth, and spat a stream of black tobacco juice straight into the open door of the stove. It sizzled. Red thought he wouldn't mind trying that, except he knew Ma would skin him alive if he ever chewed tobacco.

Red put on his cap, nodded casually and headed out, trying to still his knees, which were suddenly shaking.

He untied Flash and let him rattle along at a clipping pace. Ma was right. This was the prettiest drive on the Island. The sun was setting over the water, with swoops of reds and pinks. He felt like whooping out loud, so he did. In the distance, as if in answer, he heard the whistle of the train as it neared Applecross Station. It sounded long and encouraging. Flash suddenly sped up, and Red started to pull him back, then let him go. Flash knew the way home, for sure.

The sun had set by the time Red neared home, but it was only as he turned up his own lane in the fading light that he realized he'd clean forgotten the baking powder.

When he pulled Flash to a stop outside the barn, Mac came running out of the house.

"Ma's home!" he shouted. "She came on the train! Go on in. I'll take care of Flash."

Red leapt down and threw Mac the reins.

He burst through the back porch and into the kitchen. "Ma!"

"For mercy's sake, Red," cried Ellen. "Take off your shoes!"

But Ma just caught him up in a hug.

"How's Pa? When's he coming home?"

Some of Red's gladness at seeing Ma deflated when he saw how worn she looked. There were lines on her forehead and under her eyes that he could've sworn he hadn't seen before.

"Well, he has to stay in the hospital a few more days, the doctor said. But he'll be home by the end of next week, I hope."

"How's his—?" Red stopped.

Ma's mouth tightened with determination. "It's coming along as well as possible." She patted his back. "Ellen told me you boys finished making the caddies. That will be a real comfort to him, I'm sure."

"Hurry up and wash, Red," said Ellen, bustling over to the stove. "We've been holding supper for you." She took the casserole out of the oven. "Oh, did you get the baking powder?"

"Sorry, Ellen," muttered Red. "Slipped my mind."

Here he was trying to be all responsible, and he'd forgotten the one thing she'd asked for.

Ellen put the casserole down on the table and gave his ear a tweak. "Never mind. I daresay we won't need to bake for a while, with what the neighbours have brought over. Ma, you should see the pantry. It's near bursting."

They sat down to supper around the warm glow of the Aladdin mantle lamp, with the cats lurking under the table for scraps. It was good to have Ma home, but . . . Red looked at Pa's empty seat. Without Pa, the balance of life felt crooked, somehow. Tilted.

He suddenly remembered that when Samuel Johnson had been eight, his father had taken off and never been heard from again. Red and Mac had gone along with Ma a few times to Sam's house, with food and old clothes. The house had looked mournful, with peeling paint and crooked steps. Red had thought Mrs. Johnson always had a cold, her nose and eyes were so red. Now the house was as straight as a pin, painted a fierce yellow, and the farm was thriving under the care of Sam's Ma and his older brother and sister. Mrs. Johnson also trimmed hats for ladies in the district, in exchange for whatever they could spare. No one ever knew what became of Sam's father.

Red's knuckles tightened around his knife and fork. He couldn't imagine Pa ever really being gone.

• • •

With Ma back, Ellen opened school again on Monday. Each day, Red went to school, and each evening, he and Mac did the chores, then studied, before going to the workshop to make some more tobacco caddies. Mr. Morrison had phoned in a big new order for five hundred caddies to Gooley's store on Monday evening, and told him to pass it on to Red at school the next day. But Gooley had run over to their house right away to tell Red, and to ask after Pa, and offer to help with the caddies even though he knew nothing whatsoever about woodworking, all the while eating four of Ma's cinnamon rolls—to which Ma said never mind, because everyone knew Gooley's Ma was a dear soul but couldn't bake anything fit for the pigs.

On Thursday, a week after the accident, just before afternoon recess, the door of the schoolroom crashed open and Tommy Munn burst in.

Red's heart near stopped. Ellen gripped the edge of her desk.

"Tommy, what is it?" cried Ellen.

"Doc MacLeod." *Puff puff.* "He told me to tell yez." *Puff puff.*

"What?" said Red, springing to his feet.

"He's goin' into Charlottetown." *Puff, puff.* "Goin' to

bring yer Pa home later today." *Puff, puff.* Tommy stood there grinning and grinning.

"Tommy, for goodness' sake," snapped Ellen. "Don't you have any sense? You should know better than to burst in like that. There now, never mind. Recess."

Tommy hung around with Mac, Red and the other older boys at recess. Red thought it was some strange how Tommy prided himself on being too old for school, but not too old to kick the ball around with them.

When Ellen rang the bell at the end of recess, Tommy turned to go, his thin face streaked red from the cold. "Guess you sissies won't be stayin' on in school much longer. I guess yez'll finally have to grow up and do an honest day's work." He snorted. "Your Pa's got yez more pampered than kittens with all your schoolin'—"

"You say one more word about Pa and I'll give you something to remember." Red swung his fists.

Mac jerked him back. "Pa knows what's good for us better'n you, Tommy Munn, so don't you worry on our account. Your brain's likely taxed enough trying to remember two plus two without comin' up with five."

"Hah!" cried Tommy. "Think you're so smart."

"Smarter than you," said Mac. "But that's not hard."

Red had to jerk Mac inside as Tommy lunged at him.

But they were both silent as they hung up their coats and caps in the porch.

Red knew Mac also must have been wondering who'd have to leave school to help Pa.

That afternoon, Red found it hard to concentrate on his arithmetic. Normally it was his favourite subject, and he had no trouble adding figures, but today he just couldn't make them come out right.

It'd be best if *he* stayed home to help Pa. Mac liked school. He liked learning and was keen to become a teacher. Alex had applied for that scholarship to university and he must go if he got the chance.

Funny, though. Red wasn't crazy about school, but the thought of not being there any more gave him a strange, lost feeling. The familiar schoolroom—the pot-bellied stove, the chalkboard up front, Ellen's desk with the cracked corner, the globe on it, the pupils' desks—seemed to shift as if he were seeing it for the first time.

Everything sure had turned upside down since the day Tommy had run over to tell them about Pa's accident.

Red's fist clenched. It wasn't Tommy's fault, but part of him wanted to punch Tommy's skinny, smirking face.

When they got home after school, Ma was flying about cooking for Pa's homecoming. Her face was bright and she was starting to look like her old brisk self. Bunch ran upstairs to put on her good green skirt and white top.

Tinker, who'd cut more wood than they'd ever need all winter, and split near half of it besides, was in the kitchen.

Ma had insisted he stay for supper. His whiskers were tidy for once, his fly-away hair combed. Tinker was keen on Ma's cooking, but he seemed sombre. Even nervous.

Red and Mac hurried with their chores then changed out of their overalls and waited outside for Pa, despite the cold.

The sun had nearly set when, at last, Red heard the toot of Dr. MacLeod's car horn. Ma, Ellen and Bunch came running out.

Red was almost afraid to see Pa; he'd looked so old and tired when he'd left.

But when Pa stepped out of the car he seemed the same as ever—except for his left hand. It wasn't wrapped in a towel like before, but neatly bandaged. You could tell, though, that the last three fingers were no more than stubs.

Pa hugged Ma, Bunch and Ellen, and patted Red and Mac. "Hear you boys have been doing good work in the shop."

Pa's approving smile was all Red needed.

Old Tinker, looking ashamed, hung back.

Pa went up to him and shook his hand. "Kathleen told me how you've been helping out, Tink. I s'pose you know how grateful I am."

Tinker's eyes watered, and he muttered something Red couldn't hear.

Ma invited Dr. MacLeod to stay for supper, but he had to leave to see another patient.

"I'll look in on you tomorrow, Duncan, and change your bandage."

Red didn't watch the car head down the lane, as he normally did. He hurried inside to be with Pa.

That evening, folks started dropping in after they'd barely cleared supper. All the Munns came over, the MacMillans, Gooley's family and half of Applecross besides.

As a large crowd gathered in the sitting room, Red and Mac got up to make space for the visitors, then brought in more chairs from the parlour. Tubbs fled from the crowds in disgust, but Clover wove from leg to leg, trying to get attention. Ma and Ellen ran back and forth from the pantry serving pie and tea. Ma's lemon pies were all gone, and so was the pumpkin pie Mrs. Munn had brought, and the MacMillans' apple and raisin pies, as well as Ma's cinnamon rolls. But everyone brought more food, so there was plenty to go around.

"Well, now," said Joshua Munn, putting down his plate and leaning back, his hands across his stomach. "You be sure to let us know when you need help 'round the farm, Duncan. Though I 'spect Alex'll be comin' home to take over some of the load."

"No, I told him I want him to finish his studies," said Pa. "He might even go on to get his degree after college. He's applying for a scholarship to Dalhousie University."

Mr. Munn sucked in his lips and shook his head disapprovingly. He looked over at Mac and Red. "Well, then, I s'pose one of you smart fellas will be stoppin' home to help your Pa."

Red felt his neck go hot. It was none of Mr. Munn's business to go insinuating and suggesting.

"Oh, I think we'll manage somehow without disturbing the boys' education, Joshua," said Pa. "I've still got my thumb and one good finger. I daresay I'll never notice the others are gone." Pa leaned behind Red and picked up something from the front windowsill.

It was the trick package of gum.

"Here, now, Joshua. Have a piece of gum."

Tinker leaned forward, his eyes brightening.

Mr. Munn reached out for the gum, then yelped as the package snapped at his fingers.

There were shouts of laughter.

Pa chuckled. "Well, I guess you're lucky, Joshua. Look what it did to me." He held up his left hand with the bandaged stubs. "Guess that's what happens when you stick your fingers where they don't belong!"

For a moment there was a pit of silence.

Pa started to laugh. Ma looked as though she didn't know whether to cry or laugh, then decided to laugh. That set them all off.

Mr. Munn grinned sheepishly, and nodded.

Red hadn't realized his back had been that tight until he felt it ease. Pa was still Pa—he'd found a clever way of telling Mr. Munn to mind his own business.

And Red knew that, no matter what, Pa would make sure he and Mac got their education.

As they went to the door to say goodbye to their visitors, Pa put his bandaged hand on Red's shoulder and squeezed.

Red's eyes stung.

He'd expected a hand with fewer fingers to have less strength, but Pa's hand had the same vigour and steadiness it had always had.

It was strong enough to keep things right side up.

THE OUTHOUSE BANDIT

ON A CRISP FEBRUARY MORNING, MA HURRIED to board the sleigh beside Pa and Ellen, while Mac held onto Flash. The sun glittered blindingly off the snow. Flash snorted and pawed the snow, eager to be off.

Red handed the carpet bag to Ma, and the basket with the pies and casserole. He tucked the blankets around her and Ellen and put the heated, towel-wrapped bricks at their feet.

"Are you sure you boys will be all right?" asked Ma. "If it comes to snow, we'll have to stay the night."

"Don't worry, Ma," said Red. "We'll hold down the old fort."

He hoped Ma wasn't about to change her mind about going. A sunny Saturday like this just about begged for him to be outdoors, and it'd be easier with no one around to boss him, or insist that he study like Mac.

"We'll take care of everything, Ma," said Mac. "I'm old enough to be in charge." He shot a defiant glance at Red.

"So am I," said Red. Mac had better not forget who'd taken the lead making those caddies when Pa hurt his hand. You'd hardly know now that Pa had lost those fingers—he could do near everything with his thumb and forefinger. Funny thing was, he said he could feel the cold in the fingers that weren't there.

"Mind Bunch," said Ma. "Don't let her overfeed the cats. And be careful not to build the fire too hot. Watch out for sparks, and close that damper over before bed, but bank it so the fire doesn't go out, and—"

"Kathleen, we must get going if we're to make the funeral," said Pa. "The boys'll be fine." He turned to Red and Mac. "Be sure to consult each other, now, all right?"

Red nodded. He figured it was Pa's tactful way of saying that Mac had better not try to boss him around.

Pa clicked the reins and Flash, happy to be let loose, took off at a pace that no sensible horse would attempt through the deep snow.

Ma turned a laughing face, and called out, "Don't eat every scrap in the pantry, now. Leave something for the other pigs!"

Red grinned and waved, then headed back to the

house. All the animals had been fed and watered and the stalls cleaned. If he hurried with splitting the firewood, he could go sledding with Gooley. It had snowed on and off for most of the week, and the fields and roads were blanketed with deep, soft snow. In some places the wind had sculpted it into astonishing dunes.

It did make for a lot of shovelling, though. Red, Mac and Pa had had to clear space behind the woodshed to split firewood, and dig paths to the wellhouse and barns. The last bit of that path to Mrs. Jones's—which was behind the little barn—felt like a tunnel, with over five feet of snow on either side.

Ma had jokingly coined the term *Mrs. Jones's* for their privy; she never called it the *outhouse* because that was too coarse, she said. Red knew some of the boys in school called it far coarser names than that, and thought *privy* was highfalutin.

"We'd best top up that firewood, now," said Red. "You get some from the woodshed and I'll split."

"You get the wood," said Mac. "I'll do the splitting."

Red opened his mouth to argue but Mac interrupted, "You'd better not try calling the shots around here, Red. I'm older'n you."

"I'm just as capable, so you needn't—"

"Mac, Red!" called Bunch from the door. "Clover's spittin' up again."

143

The boys rushed to the door. Red shoved against Mac, and Mac shoved back. They stumbled into the porch and stomped the snow off their boots.

Bunch was holding Clover, whose body arched with heaves.

"Put her out," cried Mac. "Quick, now."

"What'd you give her to eat?" asked Red, rushing out of the way as Bunch ran for the door. "Didn't Ma say not to feed her too much?"

"I just gave her some old porridge with cream. It wasn't much."

"Maybe it's just a furball," said Red. "Don't worry about it, Bunch."

"You don't know if it's a furball," said Mac, with that superior air that always irked Red. "Fact is, you can't be sure."

"Well, you don't know either, so—"

"I don't want Clover getting cold out there if she's sick," said Bunch.

"She'll head for the barn," said Red. "Don't worry, Bunch. Come on in, now. Shut that door."

"No," said Mac. "Come on out and help. You can take in the kindling."

Red knew Mac was deliberately trying to contradict him. Ever since Pa's accident, Mac had been getting more and more ornery—just because Red knew more about making the tobacco caddies than Mac.

"Dress up warm, Bunch," said Mac.

Red went outside and began to bring wood from the shed against the back of the house to the chopping block.

When Mac and Bunch came out, they worked in silence, with Bunch, busy and important, carting the kindling inside. It was a help to have her there, all right, but Red wasn't about to admit it to Mac.

"There, that's enough," said Red. The box inside the kitchen was near full.

"No, we'd better take in some more," said Mac, leaning on his axe like Pa did. "If it snows again later, it'll be good to have extra."

Red squinted at the clear sky and made a scoffing sound. "Does it look like snow any time soon?"

"What do you know?" said Mac. "The almanac says it's going to snow."

"The almanac's not always—"

"Well, Pa said to cut extra, so I'm going to. If you don't want to, fine."

Red thought about taking off, but he knew if he did it would somehow give Mac the edge about who was in charge. He set his jaw.

They split the rest of the wood in silence, except for Mac trying a bit too hard to whistle.

Back inside, they'd just finished stripping off their coats and boots when someone banged on the porch door.

Henry Munn came stomping in. He was all bundled up and looked as big as a haystack. "Your Pa here?"

"No," said Mac. "He went to Bracadale for a funeral, along with Ma and Ellen. One of his cousins died."

"Too bad," said Henry. "The train's stuck over in Strathan, just past Dunvegan Road, and they're wantin' men to dig out. Me and Pa are goin' over."

Red rushed for his boots. "I'll go instead of Pa." They could use the money; the railroad paid well. Two whole dollars in cold cash for a day of digging.

"They're lookin' for *men*," snorted Henry. "They don't need lads who keeps their hands soft and sissy goin' to school all day."

Red's eyes flashed. Like Tommy, Henry liked to get in his digs about them putting education ahead of farm work—especially since Pa's accident.

Before Red could say anything back, Henry left, slamming the door behind him. Red saw him climb onto the sleigh beside Mr. Munn, and they sped down the lane.

Red dragged on an extra pair of socks and began to pull his boots on again.

"What the heck d'you think you're doing?" asked Mac.

"I'm going to help dig out that train. Henry Munn's only a bit older'n me, and I guess if Pa isn't here, I can take his place." The money would help with the hospital bill Pa had had to pay when he'd hurt his hand.

"Jumpin' Old Rory!" cried Mac. "Don't be so foolish. Henry's right. You know they only take men."

"I can dig as well as any—"

"Getting a bit above yourself, aren't you?"

"Just because you're too soft—"

"I'm not soft, I'm just not daft. Who'd keep the fire going if we both went haring off? And who'd mind Bunch?"

"You stay here, and I'll go—"

"How the deuce d'you expect to get there? By the time you slog through the snow—"

"I'm going to ski over," said Red. "You're not the only one with brains around here, so keep your nose out of it."

"It'll take you forever to ski—"

"Not if I go across the far end of the mill pond and through the woods."

"You can't do that. You know what Pa said. With all the cutting of the ice—"

"I know to avoid open water, Mac." Red buttoned up his coat and put ond his warmest woollen cap, pulling down the flaps.

"The ice is too thin to cross. Pa wouldn't want you to go. He said we're supposed to consult each other—"

"He said that so you wouldn't try to boss me—"

"He said that because he knows you're as stubborn as a mule and twice as pigheaded."

"Well, I guess it was my pigheadedness that saved our

tobacco caddy orders, so you can just get off your high horse."

Red grabbed the thick mittens and scarf Ellen had knitted him for Christmas and rushed outside to the lean-to beside the woodshed.

"Red, you come right back here," called Mac.

"Hop to heck!" shouted Red. Yanking open the lean-to door, he took out the homemade skis and poles that he and Pa had made, and the spare shovel.

Mac slammed the porch door.

Red tied the shovel onto his back with rope, then strapped on his skis.

He swished down the lane to Sprucecliffe Road, along it for a few yards, then across a series of rolling fields towards the mill pond.

At the crest of a field overlooking the pond, Red stopped to catch his breath. The pond was covered with snow, sparkling and glittering in the sun. He'd helped Pa cut ice from that pond, along with a few other farmers. It had frozen over again, but what if the ice was too thin?

Red hesitated, then set his jaw.

He wasn't going back. And he wasn't about to go around by the road, either—it would take forever to get to the train tracks. If he kept to the edge of the pond, he'd be all right. That ice had to be good and thick by now.

He'd show Mac.

Red began to ski leftward, to the far end of the pond, where he knew the water was shallow in the summer. It'd be best not to go too far to the left, because the shore was steep on the other side, and besides, he'd have to dodge his way past thick woods to get to the trail. He chose a spot that he figured would be safe to cross.

Taking a deep breath, he began to ski over the pond.

It seemed as solid as could be. Red picked up speed.

Mac was much too cautious, worrying about this, that and t'other. He probably thought that made him all grown-up and responsible, but fact was, Red was just as responsible. More. Mac was—

A crack snapped through the air.

Red's heart leapt to his mouth. He slowed down, then began to ski faster, heading towards the shallower end of the pond. Another crack rang out, then another, and from the corner of his eye, he saw snow sink behind him.

Skiing as hard as he could, Red pulled himself onto the steep shoreline, with the cracking snapping at his heels. He dragged himself to the top of the slope, his heart hammering.

There. No harm done. Even if he had fallen in, he wouldn't have drowned or anything. But it was just as well he didn't have to go home to change out of wet clothes; Mac would never get over laughing.

Red began to ski towards Taylor's wood trail. The trees grew right to the edge of the pond and it was rough going; his skis kept getting tangled in low shrubs.

"Gol darn it," muttered Red, as a branch swiped his face. He pushed and yanked his way through, until at last he reached the trail.

Turning down it, he skied as fast as he could. The trail turned and split in places, but he knew if he kept going straight, he'd soon reach the end of the woods, and then it wouldn't be long before he'd hit Dunvegan Road and be far enough along to make it easy to find the train.

It took longer than he'd expected to get through the woods. Out in the open, he paused to catch his breath. Ahead of him were swoops of snow-covered fields, fringed with stands of spruce.

Ellen always went on about how beautiful the Island was in the winter, but Red couldn't see much to admire right now. On he continued, up and down the curves of the fields, until he finally reached Dunvegan Road. He skied beside the road to the train tracks, then along the tracks, until he spied puffs of steam above the snowbank. That had to be where the train was stuck.

Red put on a spurt to reach the train. It hadn't taken him much more than an hour to get there, and from the sun's position, it looked as though it was only around mid-morning. He was still in plenty of time to help shovel out that train.

Unstrapping his skis, Red stuck them upright in the snowbank. Below, at the front of the train, the plough had shoved the snow so high that it couldn't be budged. He could see faces in the passenger cars looking up at him.

Several farmers were already digging out the snow from around the engine and plough. Some of them were from Applecross, and several from Strathan. Henry, who was shovelling at the far side, stopped to gawk at him.

Red slid down the snowbank and made his way over to Dusty MacDonald, the section lineman for that stretch of the railroad.

Dusty was a short, square man, with massive arms. Ma used to joke with him that if he were an inch or two taller he'd be a perfect cube.

"Hello, Mr. MacDonald."

Dusty turned around. "G'day, boy. What're you doin' here?"

"I've come to help dig out," said Red. "Pa's away, so I thought I'd take his place."

Henry Munn leaned against his shovel and snorted.

"Well now." Dusty scratched the back of his neck. "I'm not sayin' you won't work good, Red. But I can't go hirin' every boy comes along. Can't go payin' a man's wages to a young lad, now, can I?"

"A raw young lad," said Henry. "Soft with learnin.'"

"Mind your tongue, Henry," said Mr. Munn.

Red flushed. "I'm a hard worker, Mr. MacDonald. I—"

"I'm not doubtin' you are, Red. It's just, what're these men gonna think if I go handin' out the same wages to you?"

Red glanced at the farmers. None of them seemed about to take his part. He knew they counted on digging out the train in the winter for what money they could get. It wasn't often anyone paid real cash; times were hard.

Callum MacMillan, one of Red's neighbours, looked sympathetic, but shook his head. "Best get along home, Red."

Red licked his lips. He wasn't about to go home to hear Mac say, "I told you so."

"I'll . . . I'll work for half wages, Mr. MacDonald," he blurted. "How 'bout that?" Red saw the hesitation in the section lineman's face, and added, "I'll dig with the rest, and if you figure I haven't done a good day's work, you can decide not to pay me, if that's what you want."

"Can't say fairer than that," piped up Lefty Baker. Lefty had only one good eye, and even though he looked scrawny, he was one of the strongest men around.

At last, Mr. MacDonald nodded. "All right, then. Best get started."

Red grinned. He untied his shovel and began to dig, well away from Henry.

He went at it hard until Lefty Barker came over and muttered, "Steady now, lad. Slow down. You'll burn your-self out, rate you're goin.'"

Red was grateful for the advice as the morning wore on. He knew he couldn't have kept up that pace. He'd done plenty of shovelling around home, but there'd always been an end to it. Shovel a path from the back door to the barns. To Mrs. Jones's. To the wellhouse. But the shovel-ling here seemed to go on forever. Each time they cleared a stretch of the track, and the train backed up and pushed ahead, it wasn't long before it got stuck again.

Dusty MacDonald cursed and said the track between Dunvegan and Farrandale Road was the worst, and if it weren't for the damn government wanting to buy land from all the farmers they could, just for the votes, the damn track would never have wandered all over the place like a drunken sailor—pardon his language, and good thing there were no ladies present.

Red kept up doggedly, ignoring the snide comments Henry tossed his way. Lefty said the odd encouraging word, and after a while so did some of the other men. Every now and then, Red scrambled up the slope, got his skis and moved them along the line. Each time he won-dered how much farther they'd have to dig. He wasn't sorry he'd come or anything, it was just . . . he could've been sledding with Gooley right now. Mac and Bunch were likely toasty warm by the fire with the cats purring alongside.

At noon, Dusty brought over food from a local farm, and Red stopped with the others in the shelter of a large snowdrift. Cold ham and potatoes had never tasted so good. He gulped down the hot, sweet tea and went into the woods to relieve himself like the other men. And then, slowly, stiffly, he went back to work.

"I guess you've had enough of the diggin' by now, Red, haven't ya?" said Henry, with a smirk. "You must be some tired."

Red said nothing. He wasn't about to argue with someone who had a backside like two pigs in a blanket.

"Why don'tcha go on home," said Henry. "You done better'n I thought. Softie like you."

"Mind your own business, Henry," snapped Red.

No way in heck was he about to go home now. Not without his money. When Pa had lost his fingers, he'd had to pay Dr. MacLeod, too, not just the hospital—even though the doctor charged no more than half of what he should. Pa said he'd make it up over the summer, though, doing repairs around the doctor's house.

The afternoon wore on, and the sky frowned over with clouds, but still they continued to dig. Even after they'd shovelled through the highest drifts, Dusty insisted they keep going, because, he said, it wouldn't take long for the snow to pile up in front of the plough, and the train would get stuck yet again. They dug the track into the woods and beyond the next clearing, almost to where the line met the Farrandale Road near Geary.

At last, Dusty MacDonald called a halt to the work. The train backed up, then forced its way through the last of the snow, with the folks inside the train waving and cheering as it passed by.

"Good diggin', men," said Dusty. "I guess the train'll make it at least to the next station for now." He looked relieved. Beyond that, it would be the job of the next section lineman to clear the track if the train got stuck again.

"All right. Pay time." Dusty began to hand out two-dollar bills to each of the men.

Red waited, his arms aching. His mittens were covered with snow and ice pellets. He could barely feel his toes, they were so cold. He wished he'd never said that Mr. MacDonald could decide not to pay him if he didn't want to.

Finally, Dusty turned to Red. "I guess you dug good, boy."

Henry watched, with a grin smeared across his broad, ruddy face. "Well, now, I s'pose he dug 'bout a quarter's worth."

Red shot him an angry glance.

Mr. Munn cuffed Henry and laughed. "Don't mind him, Red. Henry's just joshin'."

"You earned your dollar, fair and square, Red," said Mr. MacDonald, handing him a one-dollar bill.

"Thank you, Mr. MacDonald." Red carefully tucked the bill into his inside coat pocket. He was glad to get that whole dollar, but he'd worked just as hard as the others. He deserved two. He couldn't fault Mr. MacDonald, though. It had been his own idea.

Mr. Munn turned to Red. "Me and Henry are gonna walk back down the track to pick up the horse and sleigh over at Gillis's barn. Be glad to give you a ride home."

Red wavered. A ride sounded awfully good. But he'd had more than enough of Henry for one day.

"Thanks, Mr. Munn," he said. "I'll ski through the woods. Won't take that long."

"You sure now, boy?" Mr. Munn glanced up at the glowering clouds. "Smell snow. Shouldn't wonder if we get a pile of it agin 'fore tonight."

"You must be plumb wore out," said Henry, for once without a grin. "Come on home with us, lad. You done better'n I expected."

Red shook his head stubbornly. He didn't need favours from the likes of Henry.

"All right, but go straight home, now," said Mr. Munn. He clapped Red's shoulder. "You're a good lad. Your Pa'll be proud of you."

Red struggled to the top of the bank and strapped on

his skis. His shoulders screamed with pain. If it hadn't been for that big galoot Henry, he'd have taken that ride. Soon as he got home he'd have to rub his arms and back with the liniment Ma kept in the pantry.

Red squinted across the fields. If he cut over to the woods in the distance, and followed the wood trail, he'd reach Sprucecliffe Road. Then he'd ski along the road and it wouldn't be long before he'd be home, sitting by the fire. Except he'd have to help first with the evening chores.

Red began to ski across the fields. His arms and shoulders felt as stiff as boards. The drifts were high in places and it was hard cutting a trail. He paused often to catch his breath. He couldn't make out how late it was, but the clouds seemed to be getting thicker and darker.

He wasn't halfway across the fields when an icy wind began to blow. It flourished and swooped, spiralling fine snow against his face. Several times, Red had to stop to peer through the gusts.

The sky was grey now, with low, heavy clouds. If only it didn't start to snow as well.

At last he reached the woods. He skirted along the edge until he spied the trail, heading off to the left.

Luckily, the trail was wide and clear of scrub. It sure was a relief to be out of that wind. He followed the twisting trail, and after a while, saw the trees ahead thin.

Red's heart plummeted as he skied out into the open. It was snowing.

Hard.

He hadn't noticed it much in the woods, but out here he could barely see past the swoops of snow.

Red peered around. He was on a road all right. It didn't look familiar, but nothing did in the winter. It had to be Sprucecliffe Road, though.

A gust of wind whipped stinging snow against his face.

Maybe he wouldn't go along the road. It was still a ways to home, and it wasn't fit for a mailbox to be out. If he took the wood trail on the other side, he'd come out near the back of the MacMillans' farm, and then he'd only have to ski across a few fields to reach home. It'd be a bit longer than going by the road, but he'd be out of the wind most of the way.

Red skied down to the lower level of the road, and up again to the gap between the trees. The wind picked up, tossing the tops of the branches, sending down scuds of snow.

Red tried to ski fast through the woods, but he was stiff and tired. Again and again—more often than he liked—he stopped to catch his breath. The wood trail was longer than he remembered. In the summer he knew every kink and turn of that trail, but with the snow it was hard to make out in places. A few times he had to turn around and go back to find it. Overhead, he could hear the wind howling. Ma, Pa and Ellen would stop the night in Bracadale, for sure. He'd have to get Mac or Bunch to rub the liniment on his back.

But at least he had the dollar for his day's work. That'd show Mac.

Red skied out into the open as the trail came to an end. The wind swooped and shrieked, blowing curtains of snow almost sideways.

Red ducked back into the shelter of the trees and leaned on his poles. It was worse, way worse than he'd expected. He could hardly see.

What should he do now? Wait in the woods until that wind died down?

No.

He couldn't wait in there getting colder and stiffer.

He knew which way to go; it wasn't far. If he just crossed the back of the MacMillans' farm, he'd spot his own house. The wind was bound to settle down—at least enough for him to see where he was going.

As if to encourage him, the wind dropped.

Red squinted at the fields ahead. He should be able to see the MacMillans' house over to the left, but he couldn't. Likely it was just the snow. The MacMillans' house was white, too.

Red took a deep breath and, putting his head down against the wind, began to ski in what he knew had to be the right direction. Even that short stop seemed to have frozen his arms and shoulders. The land dipped downward, then up. Red strained to make it to the top of the crest.

The wind settled again for a moment.

Red peered through the snow.

No house in sight anywhere.

Nothing—absolutely nothing—looked familiar.

Icy pellets of fear gathered in his stomach. Where in tarnation was he?

Before he could make sense of it, the wind shuddered and howled again, blasting snow against him.

He must keep going. He had to keep going. If he headed leftward, he'd reach home. He was bound to.

Snow stung his face, blinding him. His eyebrows and eyelashes were frozen, his hands and feet numb. His skis kept getting stuck in the drifts. Again and again he fell. He struggled to his feet each time, but he didn't bother any more to dust off his clothes.

Darn it, he should have gone with Mr. Munn. He'd have been home by now if he had. He could have put up with Henry's jokes. Pa had put up with far worse for letting them go to school. If Pa could take it, Red could, too. Even Henry's worst taunts would've been better'n being out here.

Wherever here was.

Red paused, and, covering his forehead with his arm, peered through the squalling snow.

The wind slowed long enough for Red to glimpse something—not white—in the distance to his right.

A building. It had to be a building of some sort.

A twisted sigh escaped Red's lips.

He couldn't tell if it was a house or barn, let alone whose, but that didn't matter, as long as he got out of the wind and snow. A barn would be near heaven, and warm enough with animals and hay.

Red kept his eyes on that brown smudge and skied on. But the smudge vanished as the wind whipped up again.

Gooley had told him the story of a girl who'd disappeared in the winter, a long time ago. When the snow had melted in the spring, they'd found her body, not far from home.

Red kept going, arm over arm, legs moving, heading straight towards where he'd seen that building. Then the wind dropped again, long enough for him to catch a glimpse of that brown thing—but over to his left now.

He'd been going the wrong way! He could have gone on and on . . .

Red corrected his course, even as the wind shrieked and howled, blinding him with snow. But he didn't dare stop. If he stopped he'd never be able to move again.

And then, from the corner of his eye, he saw something close by. It was lost again in the snow, but Red turned and headed straight in its direction.

And banged right into it.

Oh, thank the Lord. He'd found shelter!

He worked his way around, not daring to lift his frozen hands off the surface. It was probably a shed or a barn. He stumbled down a pile of snow as he rounded the corner of the building.

There was a path that had all but drifted in, leading to the door. With numb fingers, Red fumbled and tugged at his ski straps. At last, he managed to take them off. He stuck the skis and poles upright in the snow, then dragged open the door and went inside.

No hay. No warm animals.

It was a privy.

A privy, small and square with a wide bench built over the other side, and the one hole.

Red shut the door and tried to catch his breath. Even though it was winter, there was still a faint trace of that privy smell.

There had to be a house nearby. But whose? There was no way of telling who this privy belonged to. It wasn't the kind of thing you went around studying. In the fast-dimming light he saw there was an Eaton's catalogue on the bench, like in any other privy, and a pail of lime nearby, encrusted with frost.

Gooley's privy was the only one he'd have recognized because it was painted a bright barn-door red inside. Mr.

MacKenzie had had some of that paint left over at the end of one summer and he'd insisted on using it up—but Mrs. MacKenzie had said if he so much as laid a brush stroke of that inside her house, or in the store, she'd paint him red, so he'd gone and let the privy have it instead.

This privy had bare wood, like most of the others.

Red opened the door, but he couldn't see a thing. Despite the squalling snow, he knew it would be dark soon. He shut the door tight. He'd best stay put until the wind died down, at least enough for him to find his way. He wasn't about to go out in that storm again.

Red scrunched up in a corner, as far away from the bench as possible. The wind howled and moaned outside, pounding the privy walls.

He might have to spend the night in there.

If only he could get out again without anyone seeing him. Mac would never get over laughing, if he knew. Red would be the butt of jokes in all of Applecross. On the whole Island, for that matter.

Red wrapped his arms around his legs. Holy Moses, it was cold. Cold enough to freeze a brass monkey.

After a while, he got to his feet and began to pace up and down, slapping his arms. He stopped to do some jumping jacks, even though the muscles in his arms and legs screamed—anything to get warmed up and keep the circulation going.

He was in mid-air when the door burst open.

"Ahhh!" someone shrieked. "What the devil . . . ?"

"It's all right," cried Red. "It's only me."

Someone held up a lantern.

Red saw a big, beefy face, mouth open in alarm.

Henry Munn.

Recognition dawned on Henry's face.

"What in tarnation are you doin' here? You near scared the life right outta me."

"I got lost in the storm," said Red. "I just found this and got inside."

"Well, I never." Henry shook his head. "You must be froze."

Red nodded, his eyes suddenly stinging.

Henry clapped Red on the shoulder. "You go on outside, lad. Stand by the door. Don't go movin' anywheres. I'll be right out."

Red nodded, shamefaced. He stood out by the door in the blustering snow, then remembered to pick up his skis and poles.

Thank goodness for the wind, he couldn't hear any sounds from the privy.

At last Henry came out. "All right," he shouted. "You hold onto me. I'll hold onto the rope. Pa fixed it so's we'd find the way even in the worst storm."

A rope. If only Red had thought to look. He needn't have been found in the privy, and by Henry Munn, of all people. To think he'd skied right past the MacMillans' house, and even the back of his own, to end up here.

Holding onto Henry's back, Red followed him through the driving snow to the back door of the Munns' farmhouse, and into the porch.

Mrs. Munn, her round face flushed from the heat of the stove, stood by the kitchen table, holding a casserole dish in a towel. Her jaw dropped when she saw Red.

Mr. Munn, sitting at the table, gaped at him, along with Tommy and Clarence. Clarence was only eight, but like his older brothers, he couldn't wait to leave school.

"Found him in the outhouse," said Henry. "The lad got hisself lost."

"By the Lord liftin'!" Mrs. Munn thumped down the dish and hurried over, along with Mr. Munn.

"Was worryin' about you when that wind come up so fast," said Mr. Munn. "I shoulda insisted you come with us."

"Git your coat off this minute," said Mrs. Munn. "Henry, dust him off with the broom. Land sakes alive, you're covered in snow."

Henry swatted him with the broom and got most of the snow off. Red fumbled with his boot laces, while Mrs. Munn clucked on.

At last, in borrowed socks, Red sat down at the table with the Munns.

Henry seemed to have recovered from his fright. As he ploughed into the pork and vegetable casserole, he started to chuckle.

"Well, Red, dint know what to think when I first saw ya. Thought you was a ghost. Or a bandit, or sumpin." He rumbled with laughter. "Don't look to find nobody in the outhouse when you go answer a call of nature."

"A bandit!" Tommy's grin just about cracked his bony face. "A bandit in the poo-palace!"

Mrs. Munn wagged a finger at him. "Don't want to hear no such talk from you, Tommy."

"All right, stink-house, then."

"It's *outhouse*, Tommy!" said Mrs. Munn, swatting at him.

"All right, all right," said Tommy, ducking. "A bandit in the outhouse."

Clarence sniggered. "What would he be tryin' to steal in there?"

"Well, now," said Henry. "He's a fine scholar, aren't you, Red? I'm guessin' he run out of readin' material in his own outhouse. Wanted to catch up on his readin' at the neighbours."

Red gritted his teeth and shot Henry an uncharitable glance.

"Don't mind them," said Mrs. Munn, chuckling. "The boys is only havin' a bit of fun."

The supper wore on with the boys' jokes getting sillier and more exaggerated. By the end of the meal, Red was so warm, his ears felt like they were on fire.

It was funny, he thought, how life twisted on you, like a stormy wind. He'd been too proud to ride home with the Munns for fear of Henry's taunts, and now here he was, with all three of the Munn boys taking a turn at him, and he couldn't even say anything back. He was in their kitchen, eating their food. Glad of their warmth.

After supper was cleared, Red realized that the wind wasn't howling any more, just whistling now and then. He looked out and saw that the snow had stopped. It was dark outside, but with the whiteness of the snow, he knew he'd find his way home all right; he could even see his own lighted kitchen window from there.

"Thanks for the supper, Mrs. Munn. Guess I'd best be getting home."

"I'm not lettin' you head off alone," said Mr. Munn.

"Don't worry," said Henry, grinning. "I'll get the Outhouse Bandit home. Can't have him wanderin' around, tryin' outhouses. Scarin' decent folk."

"Cut it out!" snapped Red.

"Outhouse Bandit!" crowed Tommy.

Henry, Clarence and Tommy guffawed.

And Red knew that by Monday everyone in school would be calling him that. He cringed at the thought of Shona Murray hearing the tale and laughing. He'd rather she didn't know he existed.

"No harm intended, lad," said Henry. "I'm real glad you're safe an' sound." He thunked his paddle of a hand on Red's back.

Henry harnessed the horse to the sleigh and drove Red home. Tommy insisted on coming along.

When they reached Red's house, Tommy insisted on accompanying Red to the back door.

Red knew exactly why—Tommy wasn't done having fun.

As Red pushed open the door, Mac came hurrying into the porch with a lantern.

"Where the dickens were you?" said Mac.

Red stomped his feet to shake off the snow. "Got lost coming home," he muttered. "Had to stop at the Munns' until the storm ended."

"In the outhouse, as a matter of fact," chortled Tommy. "Your brother's a right smart one. He likes to read somethin' fierce. Henry found him readin' the catalogue in there—"

"I wasn't!"

Mac looked from Tommy to Red.

"You'd best keep an eye on him," continued Tommy,

wagging his head. "Can't have him wanderin' 'round, tryin' out neighbours' outhouses, scarin' 'em half to death. Outhouse Bandit!"

Red pulled off his mittens, hung up his scarf and cap and unlaced his boots.

Mac would never let him forget this. He'd crow, and assert his older-and-smarter brother status.

"If he gits a hankerin' for reading material," continued Tommy, "best direct him to—"

"Shut it, Tommy," said Mac. "That's enough."

Red jerked around.

Tommy opened his mouth to say something but Mac forged on, "At least Red had the sense to find shelter and stay put. You'd probably have wandered off and got yourself killed."

Tommy snorted. "I wouldn't have ended up in no outhouse."

"You wouldn't have had the gumption to find it, in the first place," said Mac.

"Ha, ha, think you're so funny."

"Funnier than you. But that's not hard."

"Now look here," said Tommy, putting up his fists. "I just brung your brother back, but if you're lookin' for a fight, I'll give you one."

Mac put up his fists, too. "I'm not afraid of you, you big—"

"Stop it," said Red, shoving his way between them. "You're not fighting in here."

Tommy stepped back, shamefaced. "Well, your brother better not go callin' me names."

"Then stop calling my brother names," said Mac.

Tommy and Mac stared at each other, neither willing to look away first.

"Tommy, you'd best get going," said Red. "Henry's waiting out in the cold. Tell him thanks for bringing me home."

Muttering, Tommy left.

Red started to hang up his coat, then dug his hand inside the pocket and found the dollar bill. He handed it to Mac. "That's what they paid me."

"A dollar," said Mac.

Red waited for Mac to say that was half the normal rate, but Mac didn't. He just put the dollar bill on the kitchen table and weighed it down with Ma's package of trick gum.

Red went over to the stove and rubbed his hands at the warmth. The cats were curled up nearby. Clover lifted her head to peer at him, then snuggled down to sleep again.

"Where's Bunch?" asked Red after a while.

"In bed."

Red pulled his chair closer to the stove. He watched the steam rise from the bottom of his pants. He thought about all the things Mac could say. How Red had been so puffed up about the tobacco caddies, he'd thought he knew it all. How, if Red hadn't been so proud and stubborn, he'd never have got himself in such a mess. And how, when Pa had said they should consult each other, maybe he'd meant it just as much for Red as for Mac—maybe more.

But Mac didn't say a word. He just began to whistle tunelessly.

The fire hissed and spat.

"Pa'll be glad of the dollar, I expect," said Mac.

Red cleared his throat. "I'm ... well ... I'm sorry if you were concerned about me."

"Wasn't the least concerned. Knew you'd be fine." Mac stretched out his legs.

There was a thudding sound as a log slipped inside the stove.

A small grin crept across Mac's face. "Mind you, I didn't expect you'd end up in a privy."

Red shot Mac a sharp glance. But Mac didn't look like he was gloating.

"Well," said Red, "I guess I didn't either."

Mac whistled some more. Tubbs woke up, yawned mightily, then started to groom himself.

"You should've seen Old Henry's face," said Red, "when he opened that door and saw me." He let his jaw fall slack and his eyes go wide.

Mac hooted with laughter, along with Red.

Red's laughter faded into a groan. "You know what they're going to call me in school, don't you? Outhouse Bandit." He groaned again.

"Well, who says you've got to just take it?" Mac blinked hard. "You can say how terrified old Henry was when he saw you." He leaned forward, a gleam in his eyes. "You could say he wet himself!"

Red lifted his head.

"For that matter, you could say he even soiled his pants."

Red almost fell to the floor laughing.

When they stopped laughing, Red got the liniment from the pantry and Mac helped rub it onto his back and shoulders.

The warmth was bliss on his aching muscles, but Red knew that he'd be sore for a while.

And the butt of jokes in school for even longer.

But at least . . . at least he wouldn't be alone.

Mac would be right there, with him.

And together, they'd give as good as they got.

THE EDGE OF THE WORLD

ALEX, RED AND MAC ERUPTED FROM THE WOOD trail into the blazing sunshine, and raced down the pasture field to the sparkling blue ocean.

"Last one in mucks out the pig barn," roared Alex.

Red pumped his arms and sprinted across the shore field, his eyes fixed on the gleaming water. He tore off his shirt, scrambled and slipped over the edge of the field onto the sand. Shouting and laughing, he kicked off his shoes, whipped off the rest of his clothes and plunged into the water—behind Alex, but just ahead of Mac.

The coldness of the water made him gasp, but as soon as he was in deep enough, Red dove under.

"I beat. I beat," he shouted as he surfaced. "Mac, you're cleaning the pigsty!"

Mac caught up and splashed him, protesting that technically he'd been ahead, because Red hadn't taken off one of his socks. They argued and laughed about it, until Alex ruled that Red had won fair and square, and Mac had better clean out the pig barn.

"But next time socks off, or you're it, Red," said Alex, grinning.

Red pulled off his sock, balled it and threw it to shore. He ducked down, washing off the chaff and grime of the day, then eased onto his back, floating.

It didn't get much better than this, cooling off in the Northumberland Strait with his brothers.

They'd been haying with Pa all week, and busier than toads eating grubs. They'd cut the hay, let it dry on the ground for a few days, then forked it into coils. The coils had been left to dry a couple more days, then loaded into the wagon to put in the hayloft.

It had been hot as blazes, even for late July, and they'd been hard at it every single day. Earlier that afternoon, when they'd done filling the hayloft, they'd built a neat haystack, near the barn, to be used in the winter. Then Pa had said, seeing as how they'd worked so hard, and since Tinker was over to help, they could take the rest of the afternoon off and go for a swim.

It took near an hour to jog and walk through the wood trails and fields to the shore at Sandy Point, but it sure was worth it.

Red paddled around lazily. Not a cloud in the sky.

Blue, blue water, green fields sloping down to golden sands and red cliffs jutting out like the arms of the land were reaching out to hold them safe. Red dunked his head under. Holy Moses, the sun must've made him right soft in the head, thinking such poetical stuff.

Alex stared at the hazy horizon.

"Not too many days you can't see Nova Scotia," he said. "But I guess I'll be there soon enough."

"Did you get word about your lodgings?" asked Mac.

Red turned and splashed noisily away from his brothers.

Why did they have to go spoil things every time? Why did they have to keep talking about going away?

Red was proud that Alex had won a scholarship to Dalhousie, the big university on the mainland, but when he thought of Alex leaving—not just for Charlottetown, but off the Island—he felt a dull tightness in his chest.

And Mac! He wasn't even going to college in Charlottetown 'til the fall of next year, but he kept talking about it, as though . . . as though he and Alex belonged to a grown-up world in which Red hadn't any part.

Over the winter, when Red had taken the lead making the tobacco caddies, he'd thought he'd caught up to Mac—but here he was, the youngest again. On the edge of his brothers' world.

On the edge of everyone's world.

Ma and Ellen were busy too, sewing up a storm for Ellen and Stew's wedding after the harvest; Granny had postponed her usual summer visit to the Island, so she could be there for it. Ellen wasn't moving far—only to Clearwater—but she'd be teaching somewhere else, and there'd be a new teacher in Applecross.

Seemed like everything was changing. Too fast.

Red ducked under and swam towards his brothers' legs, waving about like eels. He grabbed and pulled.

Spluttering, laughing, Mac and Alex chased him and dragged him under.

When they were tuckered out, they floated peaceably, enjoying the sun.

At last, Alex said, "Best be getting home. Don't want Ma to hold supper on us."

"And you have to do the pigsty, Mac," crowed Red. He was some glad to get out of that task—the sty was over-due for cleaning.

They headed back to shore, shook themselves dry and got dressed.

As they walked home through the wood trails, Alex began to tell Mac about the courses he hoped to take at university, and about his plans to work over the summer so he'd be able to pay for Mac's education. Ellen had said she'd spot him the money if he needed it, and he could pay her back when he got a fat job with his degree.

Red lengthened his stride and outstripped them. Their voices burbled on behind him, as if they didn't even notice he wasn't around.

The delicious coolness from the swim soon faded— it was one of those rare Island evenings without much of a breeze. Red grew warmer and warmer as he trudged across Callum MacMillan's back pasture field, it was a narrow strip stretching across the back of the MacMillan, MacRae and Munn farms, all the way to Berryfield Road.

The drone of his brothers' voices became fainter . . . and then began to grow into a muttering rumble.

It took Red a few seconds to register that throaty sound. His head jerked up.

"Alex, Mac," he shouted. "Look. An aeroplane."

Shielding his eyes with his hand, he stared at the aeroplane coming into view. It was bright red. A glorious Gipsy Moth.

The roar of the plane deepened, then sputtered.

"Something's wrong," said Red. "It doesn't sound right." He knew exactly what it should sound like—the mail plane from Halifax to Charlottetown flew over their farm every day.

The aeroplane was overhead now, sputtering louder as it flew lower along the length of the field.

"He's looking for somewhere to land!" said Red.

He began to sprint across the field as the plane turned to head into the wind. By the time he reached the edge, more people had come running into the field—Callum and Moira MacMillan with their two boys, and their pesky nine-year-old daughter, Erica, as well as several other folks. Everyone stopped to watch as the plane waggled its wings, then came in towards the field.

"He's landing here," cried Red.

"Holy mackerel," hooted Erica MacMillan, jumping up and down, her dark, tangled hair bouncing.

"Everyone, get out of the way," shouted Callum. He grabbed Erica as she tried to run into the field.

The aeroplane came lower and lower. It touched down, bounced up and down a few times, and finally stayed down.

The plane began to slow, then the sound of its sputtering engine died, and at last the plane came to a stop, with the skid of its tail resting against the ground.

Red raced towards it, ahead of the others. The plane had stopped near the fence and hedgerow separating the MacMillans' field from the back of his own farm.

"Didja see that? Didja see that?" yelled Gooley, running behind him. "Holy Moses, that was sumpin.'"

Red reached the plane first, followed by Alex, Mac, Gooley, Clarence Munn and Erica. He saw yet more folks come running into the field: Pa, Ma, Bunch and Ellen were among them. It looked as though more than half the people in Applecross were there.

Gasping, Red stopped near the wing of the plane along with the others.

The pilot pushed his goggles back on top of his leather helmet and climbed out onto a narrow strip of the wing that was painted black, adjacent to the cockpit.

Red rushed to help him, but the pilot jumped to the ground unaided.

Red could hardly take it all in—the magnificent aeroplane and the splendid pilot, a real live pilot who could fly it.

He couldn't think of a word to say. All he could do was gawk and grin, and grin and gawk.

The plane was a Gipsy Moth, as he'd thought, a two-seat biplane, and it wasn't even all fabric; the cowl was metal. The pilot wore brown pants and boots and a leather jacket. Red had never seen anyone who looked like that outside of pictures in books.

Callum MacMillan, who was tall, thin and mild-mannered, held out his hand and introduced himself. "I guess you ran into some problems, going over. Glad my field was obligin' enough to be here for you. And that my cows and horses are in the other pasture."

The pilot shook hands. "Matthew Tompkins. I'm awfully grateful to you. I was desperate for a flat field without livestock."

He didn't have an Island accent, Red noticed. He was from away. Of course he was from away. You didn't associate something like flying with any ordinary Islander, although there was a flying club that had opened not long ago, over in Charlottetown.

But Red felt a twinge of disappointment that the pilot wasn't tall. Mr. Tompkins was a good head shorter than Mr. MacMillan, who was a six-footer. Pilots, he'd thought, should tower above ordinary folks.

Mr. Tompkins smiled, his blue eyes scanning the crowd. "Howdy, folks. My apologies for coming down unexpectedly." He pulled off his helmet and brushed his hand across his forehead.

Red felt another twinge of disappointment. Mr. Tompkins was middle-aged. He had sandy red hair with a receding hairline and a crooked nose, and his face and hands were freckled just like Pa's. He sure didn't look like the pictures Red had seen in *The Boy's Own Annual* of pilots who'd fought in the war. They were always young, handsome and tall. With a full head of hair.

Mr. Tompkins smiled again, a gold tooth glinting in the corner. He began to shake hands with everyone, even the children.

Red could hardly believe that a real pilot, who flew about in the skies, would want to shake hands with children. Bunch squirmed through next to Red and grinned as Mr. Tompkins pumped her hand, too.

Pa, along with a few others, started to ask Mr. Tompkins about the plane and what they could do to help. Red liked that Mr. Tompkins didn't go staring at Pa's left hand with its three missing fingers, the way some folks did.

"It's the magneto again," said Mr. Tompkins, wiping his forehead with the back of his hand. "A coil shorted out. I'm afraid I'll have to send to Charlottetown for it. I wonder if I can board with someone here until it comes in?"

"You can stay with us," Erica MacMillan hollered. "Can't he, Pa? He landed in our field so he has to stay with us. Tell him."

Red burned with frustration that he hadn't thought to ask. After all, the pilot had landed along the back of their farm, and his plane was closer to their house than to the MacMillans'.

Everyone began to talk at once, offering advice on how to get the part that the pilot needed, some asking him to drop by for tea, or dinner or supper. Red tried to edge closer, but Erica, with her mop of hair, kept getting in the way.

"You can use our telephone to call for the part," said Gooley. "We've got one at the store."

"We've got one too," chimed Clarence Munn. "And it's closer."

Gooley elbowed Clarence out of the way. "But ours is in the store and it's the one everyone uses if they don't have a phone. And anyway, Mr. Tompkins might need some supplies if he's to stay here."

The pilot laughed, and said, "I guess I will."

Gooley grinned from ear to ear, while Clarence scowled.

Red gritted his teeth. If they'd had a phone, the pilot could have come to *their* house.

Then Pa spoke up. "Likely the easiest way for you to get the part is to have them send it down by train. It'll be the quickest and most reliable. The Applecross Station's just down the road."

Mr. Tompkins looked relieved, and Red puffed with pride that Pa had actually offered real advice instead of prattling on foolishly like the rest of them.

"Thank you, Mr. MacRae," said Mr. Tompkins. "The train will be just the ticket. Soon's I get the coil, the old girl and I can be on our way."

The old girl. Red stared at Mr. Tompkins. He talked about his aeroplane as if it were a real person. Imagine having that kind of bond with a plane! As though it were something ordinary, like a . . . like a horse. But Red saw Mrs. Munn purse up her lips, and Ma and a few other women looked disapproving.

Red shoved Erica aside to catch the grown-up conversation better. He heard that the pilot had been in

Charlottetown, giving lessons at the new flying club. He'd been heading to Nova Scotia to visit friends, before going home to Ontario, when the engine had started to sputter.

"Now, if you don't mind, I'll have to get the old girl tied down. I have my ropes and tarps, but I'm afraid I don't have the anchors for the ropes. I wasn't expecting to stop in a field." He looked around. "I'm going to need some big rocks, or some stakes—"

"I'll get the stakes," shouted Red, before anyone else could speak. "I'll get them from the workshop. We're the closest. D'you need anything else, sir?" He flushed to the roots of his hair when he saw Alex and a few others look at him, and realized that he'd yelled just like a little kid.

The pilot turned to him and smiled. "Thanks, young man."

"It's Red, sir."

"Well, thanks, Red. That would be just the ticket."

Red raced across the field, over the pasture fence and through the hedgerow separating the MacMillans' farm from theirs. He sped along the edges of a succession of fields, through a gate, across the stubble of the hayfield and through another gate to the backyard, and finally into the workshop in the little barn. He had to get those stakes before anyone else did—he wanted *his* stakes to hold down the plane.

Red found the wooden stakes—thank goodness Pa kept a tidy shop, with everything in place—ran out, then doubled back to get the hammer.

He could hardly breathe by the time he returned to the edge of the crowd that surrounded the plane.

"'Scuse me," he puffed. The crowd parted for him, like he was someone important. But it was the pilot's smile that mattered.

Everyone hurried around to help. Red, along with Pa and a few others, helped the pilot thread the rope through the metal loops at the front of the fuselage and stake them to the ground. They threaded more rope through the loops below the lower wings, just under the struts, and also hammered them into the ground. Then they covered the cockpit with the tarp, and staked it, too. Mr. Tompkins went around checking to make sure everything was good and tight.

"Thanks, Red," said Mr. Tompkins.

Red grinned. "You're welcome, sir."

The pilot took a few large rocks from the edge of the field and positioned them on either side of the wheels.

"There. She'll be safe and sound 'til I get her fixed." He turned to the children clustering around and made his face solemn. "I hope you young people understand that you must never touch this aeroplane without me here. Is that clear?"

Everyone nodded. Red gave Erica MacMillan a long, hard stare. He bet that pesky kid didn't understand how valuable a plane was. He'd have to keep an eye on her.

"Now then," said Mr. Tompkins. "Where can I get hold of a phone?"

"Over at the store." Gooley pushed his way forward. "Come with me, sir."

Strutting, Gooley led the way down the length of the pasture, towards Berryfield Road, with the crowd trailing behind. Red felt a little irked at how Gooley thrust his chest out. Gooley had better not forget it was Red's stakes that held the plane down. They went down to the crossroads—with Clarence pointing out that his house was really closer—and over to MacKenzie's store.

A few of the men went inside with the pilot, while the rest of the crowd waited outside, talking over every detail of the landing, and arguing over who'd seen the plane first. Red knew he had, although Erica insisted she'd been the first to spot it.

When the pilot came back out, he said, "They'll send the part by train in a day or so."

"You're staying with us," shouted Erica. "You've got to stay with us. You promised. Pa, tell him."

Mr. Tompkins laughed. But when Mr. and Mrs. MacMillan echoed the offer, he accepted with thanks.

Red walked back with them along Sprucecliffe Road,

with Clarence once again pointing out, as they passed the Munns' house, how it would have been quicker to have phoned from his place.

Red reluctantly followed his family up the lane to his own house, while the MacMillans continued with the pilot to their farm. He wondered what the pilot was talking about now.

"Best get the chores done before supper today, boys," said Pa. "It's gettin' late, and the cows need to be milked."

Red trailed Pa and his brothers to bring the cows in from pasture. Mac seemed relieved that he didn't have time to clean the pigsty that evening, until Alex said he'd be sure to remind him the next day.

When they got back to the house after the chores, Ma set about getting supper. They sat down to eat, still talking about the astonishing events of the afternoon. The first chance he got, Red asked if they could have the pilot over for a meal.

"We'll see," said Ma. "We've enough to do with all the farm work and Alex leaving. Oh, my!" She put her hand to her mouth. "I nearly forgot. Alex, your suit is here from Eaton's." Ma went into the sitting room and came back with new pants and a jacket, made out of grey wool.

"Ma, it's too much," said Alex. He tried on the jacket and smoothed the lapel. "However did you manage it, with Ellen's wedding coming up and all."

"Don't worry, Alex." Ma beamed. "We had a good bit of credit at the store, thanks to the caddies, so I used my egg and cream money to send for the suit from the catalogue." She dusted a speck off his arm. "We couldn't let you go off to Nova Scotia in tatty old clothes. You'll need it for Ellen's wedding, anyway."

Red felt himself crash down to earth. Alex seemed so fine and grown-up in that suit. Almost like a stranger who didn't belong in Applecross.

"Take good care of it, Alex," said Mac. "I'll be gettin' it in a couple of years." He punched Red's arm. "Alex always gets new, and Red too, because everything's too worn after I'm done. Seems like I'm always the one with hand-me-downs."

"Oh, you poor thing!" Ellen twisted Mac's ear. "Barely a thread to wear! And I made you two new shirts myself."

"Best take off your fine new duds, Alex," said Pa, smiling. "I guess it's a bit too fancy for the cows—those ladies won't much appreciate it."

"Unlike others," said Ellen, laughing.

Alex grinned and shook his head. There'd always been lots of girls in Applecross keen on Alex, and more so since he'd come back from Charlottetown with the air of a city boy. Now, with the glamour of the mainland looming, it seemed like they were clean crazy over him. He, on the other hand, didn't seem taken with any of them, to Red's secret relief.

Red found it hard to settle down to anything that evening. He felt itchy and restless. Sort of pulled between the upward lift of the plane's landing, and the downward crush of Alex leaving.

• • •

It rained the next morning, but when it cleared up in the afternoon, Red helped Pa weed the turnips and potatoes. He and Mac took their turn sitting on Jean's broad back to guide her between the drills. Pa and Alex took turns steadying the scuffler from behind, to keep the teeth that dug up the weeds from damaging the crops.

Red's thoughts kept flying to the plane in the pasture field. When would the magneto coil come in? He and Gooley had made a pact that if either of them heard, they'd tell the other. There was no way on this good green earth that Red was going to miss seeing that plane take off. He'd never seen one take off before.

A shiver worked its way along Red's spine. He was some glad to be living in the modern times, in a world with aeroplanes. It was hard to imagine that, for most of his life, Pa had never even seen a car, never mind a plane.

When they were done weeding, Ma came out and told them they'd best take care of the livestock before supper because they'd be eating later that evening. Red helped his brothers with the rest of the chores, then ambled over to the wellhouse to pump a bucket of water to take back to the house. He wondered why Ma was behind with supper; he was so hungry his belly was flapping.

As he entered the porch, Ma turned around, smiling. "Wash up nice and good, now. We have company coming for supper."

"Who?"

"Mr. Matthew Tompkins. I went over earlier today to see how he was doing and asked him to supper. Just beat a few other ladies to it, too."

Red whooped. "Thanks, Ma."

Ma laughed and shook her head. "Well, I didn't think I'd get any peace from you until I did invite him. That man is being near smothered with invitations. I daresay that aeroplane won't be able to lift off, he'll be so fat from all the eating. Go and get Alex and Mac. Tell them to hurry on in. Oh, Honey-Bunch, keep your fingers out of that pie filling."

Bunch turned away from the lemon pie. "I was only checking to see if it's good enough for Mr. Matthew."

Red hooted. "That's Mr. Tompkins, Bunch!"

Bunch glowered at him. Red ruffled her hair and raced

back to the wellhouse, where Mac and Alex were standing around, still jawing away.

"Hurry! The pilot's coming to supper. Ma said you'd better clean up quick."

He raced back to the kitchen, dipped up some hot water from the tank beside the stove, washed thoroughly, then ran upstairs to change into his good clothes, without Ma even telling him.

Red swung his arms as he watched for Mr. Tompkins from the front sitting room window. The potatoes that Pa had planted in the front field this year were thick and bushy, the red blossoms mostly faded. The field on the other side of the lane, where they'd grown hay last year, was now a pasture. Across the road he could see Mr. Nicholson forking his cut hay into coils.

Red near jumped out of his skin when someone knocked on the back door. Mr. Tompkins had come across the back fields, like any of the MacMillans might. Like any ordinary person in Applecross.

Red raced across the length of the room to the kitchen.

"Well, hello again, young man," said Mr. Tompkins, holding out his hand. He wore a regular white shirt with brown pants, and he looked for all the world like any normal person.

"Hello, sir." Red couldn't think of another word to say.

Luckily, the others weren't so tongue-tied. As they sat

down to supper, Red listened hard to the conversation. Mr. Tompkins, it turned out, had been in the war and had flown reconnaissance missions.

"The war!" cried Red, his tongue unleashed. "That must have been something. Wish I'd been there to see the fun."

Mr. Tompkins whipped around, his eyes hard.

Red froze.

"It wasn't fun, Red. Don't you ever go thinking that. There were young lads, Alex's age, and younger, who lied to get in. A lot of them were killed or maimed. You've no idea what it was like." The anger in Mr. Tompkins's face faded. He looked plain tired. "There's nothing fun about a war, let me tell you."

Red didn't know what to say. But he saw Ma look at the pilot with respect.

"I hope we never have to go through anything like that again," she said.

"Amen," said Mr. Tompkins. He bent down to pet Clover, who was sitting at his feet, then glanced at Red. "Didn't mean to snap at you, young man. It's just . . . well, I guess I had such ideas too, when I joined up. Didn't take long to become disillusioned, let me tell you." He smiled. "The flying, though. I could never get enough of it. I sure loved being up in the sky, looking down on the earth. It's an amazing sight . . . maybe that's why after the war I had to keep flying."

Red leaned forward. "The engine, sir. How does it work?"

Ellen clicked her tongue. "Don't go pestering Mr. Tompkins, now, Red."

"I don't mind," said Mr. Tompkins. "It's a pleasure to talk to a young man so bright and interested."

Red thought he'd just about burst with pride. He listened eagerly as the pilot tried to explain the intricacies of aeroplane engines. By the time the pilot finished, Red figured he knew a good bit about them, and even about the body of the plane. Mr. Tompkins explained how the fabric was doped so it was waterproof and windproof, and Red thought he understood most of it.

"When the part comes in," said Mr. Tompkins, getting up to leave, "maybe you can help me fix the plane, Red. Be my assistant. Hand me wrenches, and so on."

Red's face glowed. "I'll be there even if it's the middle of the night."

Ma burst out laughing.

"That's not likely, Red," said Ellen, twisting his ear.

They all went to the back door to wave goodbye to the pilot.

At bedtime, as Red went up to the loft with Alex and Mac, he shut out their conversation about college and university. He climbed into bed, pretending he was on that plane.

He wished he could be up there in the sky, rather than down here, plodding on the earth.

• • •

The magneto coil for the aeroplane wasn't on the train the next day. But when Red had a moment, after helping Ma weed the vegetable garden, he slipped over to the MacMillans' field to make sure the tarp was still on and the ropes anchoring the plane were good and tight.

The next afternoon, Red was in the far field with Alex and Mac, helping Pa thin the turnips, when Gooley came running over.

"The part came in just now," he yelled. "Mr. Tompkins says he'll fix the aeroplane tomorrow mornin' and then take off."

"D'you think you could spare me, Pa?" asked Red. "Just for the morning?" He knew the work at hand was never-ending, but he had to see that aeroplane take off.

Pa smiled. "Oh, sure, Red. I don't s'pose any of us wants to miss it. I expect we'll all be in the field to watch Mr. Tompkins."

Red could hardly sleep all night, thinking about it.

• • •

Bright and early the next morning, as soon as he heard Pa lighting the stove downstairs and putting on the porridge, Red sprang out of bed. He rushed through the milking and the other morning chores with Mac and Alex, then asked Pa if he could go over to the aeroplane.

Pa nodded. "I'll come by soon, myself."

Red sprinted between the fields to MacMillans' back pasture. He was the first one there. He circled the plane a few times before Gooley arrived, followed by Mac, Alex and others. Pretty soon there was a fair crowd in the field.

Then Red saw Shona Murray coming down the length of the pasture. He looked at her, then away. Shona's older sister, Margaret, batted her eyes at Alex, who never even noticed.

At last the pilot came down the field from the back of the MacMillans' farm. Erica ran beside him, chattering non-stop.

Red scowled. He bet Mr. Tompkins had had more than a bellyful of her.

"Well, good day, folks." The pilot smiled. "Hello, Red."

Red grinned and grinned that the pilot had singled him out.

"All right," said Mr. Tompkins. "Could everyone step back, please, and give me some space to work."

Red, along with a few others, helped the pilot take off the tarps and untie the ropes from the fuselage.

Mr. Tompkins climbed into the rear cockpit and took out a black toolbox, about the size of a breadbox.

"Now then, Red, if you'll come over and hand me the tools," he said.

Red pushed his way past Erica and stood by at the ready. He watched, enthralled, as Mr. Tompkins unlatched one side of the metal cowling at the nose of the aeroplane and lifted it back. Red stared at the coils and wires of the engine.

Mr. Tompkins got started. He pointed to the tools he needed and Red handed them over. He hoped that Shona would notice how quickly and competently he gave the pilot what he asked for. Mr. Tompkins whistled a lilting tune as he fixed the engine, as if it were an ordinary job he hardly had to think about. Red was so absorbed watching him that everything and everyone else faded, even Shona. It wasn't until the new coil was safely in place, and the pilot swung down and latched the metal cowling, that Red saw how large the crowd was around them.

Mr. Tompkins put away the toolbox. He slipped on his leather jacket and helmet and pulled on his goggles, transforming himself from an ordinary middle-aged man into a glamorous pilot.

"All right, I'm going to take the plane up for a spin, just to make sure everything's working. And then . . ." He looked around and smiled. "Well, if anyone wants to go up, I'll give you a ride at a discount rate. Five dollars. I'd offer it free if I could, you folks have been so kind, but I have to cover my costs."

Erica squealed with excitement, but Mrs. MacMillan, a slight woman with a tired face, laughed and said, "No, Erica. You're too small."

Five dollars. Red swallowed. The desire to go up was so fierce, it felt like a volcano inside him.

But he couldn't ask Pa for five dollars.

"I need someone to prop the plane for me, when I get in," said Mr. Tompkins.

Before Red could come forward, Mr. MacMillan said, "Show me what to do."

Mr. Tompkins explained that he'd get into the cockpit, stand on the brakes and get Mr. MacMillan to swing the propeller to start up the engine.

"I want everyone to stay good and clear of the propeller," said Mr. Tompkins. "And give me space to take off. And when I land, I don't want anyone near the plane before the propeller comes to a complete stop. Understood?"

The pilot climbed into the rear cockpit. He lowered the goggles over his eyes and gave Mr. MacMillan the thumbs-up.

Mr. MacMillan swung the propeller around. He had to do it three times before the engine caught. He ran out of the way, as everyone shouted and cheered.

"Move aside, now," called out Pa. "Give the pilot space to take off."

The aeroplane began to run down the field, faster and faster. The tail lifted off the ground and then the whole plane rose into the air. The engine made a wonderful throaty roar, fading to a satisfying rumble, then a purr, as the plane flew higher and higher and farther and farther away. Soon it was just a speck in the sky, but it grew bigger again as the plane circled around and came back.

Red, his eyes fixed on the plane, heard people talking about whether they'd go up for a ride. He was surprised to hear Shona say she wished she could go. Glancing back, he saw her gazing wistfully at the plane. It wasn't likely that her Pa could afford it, though. He was still taking whatever odd jobs he could get. They'd only just moved from that cabin at the back of the mill to a small house on Dunvegan Road.

Red heard Ma and Pa whispering, and saw Ellen head back home across the field. He didn't know how she could bear to miss even a minute of the flight.

Pa came over and put his hand on Red's shoulder. "Want to go up for a ride?"

Red's mouth dropped open. For a moment he couldn't speak.

Then he managed to gasp, "But the money?"

"You needn't worry about that." Pa smiled. "You worked hard over the winter with the tobacco caddies. I guess we can spring for this. It'll be a good learning experience."

Red's heart felt like it would burst clean out of his chest. He let out a whoop, then caught himself. "But . . . what about Alex and Mac?"

"Well, you're the one most hankerin' after it," said Pa. "I figure it'll mean more to you."

"It's all right by me," said Mac, shrugging. "Can't say I'm overly keen."

"Me neither," said Alex, flashing a grin.

Red could hardly believe it. He was going to go up in an aeroplane!

He was actually going to go up in that aeroplane!

As the plane came in to land, he saw Ellen hurrying back across the field. She handed Pa a wrinkled five-dollar bill, then smiled at Red and twisted his ear.

When the plane came to a stop, the pilot climbed out. "Well? Any takers for a ride?"

"Me, sir." Red stepped forward. He'd expected there'd be a rush of other folks wanting to go up, even if it did cost five dollars, but only Cynthia Johnson, Sam's older sister, said she'd like to try it. Apart from Erica, of course, who cried when the pilot agreed with her mother that she was too small.

"Well, looks like the Outhouse Bandit's goin' up to the sky," said Henry Munn, a grin across his cabbage-broad face. "Yez wouldn't catch me goin' up in that thing if yez paid me." A lot of other people muttered and nodded.

"Just as well, Henry," shouted someone. "That thar thing wun't have the chance to git off the ground if you wuz in it!"

Everyone roared with laughter, Henry loudest of all.

"All right, Red." Mr. Tompkins climbed onto the wing and, leaning into the forward cockpit, brought out a leather helmet and goggles. "Put these on."

Red put on the leather helmet, and fastened it under his chin. He just about burst with pride as he slipped on the goggles.

"Now, listen carefully," said Mr. Tompkins. "You climb on the wing, but only on the black part. Nowhere else, or you'll go straight through and we won't be flying at all."

From behind, someone joked, "Good thing Henry's too 'fraid to go up—he'd have that thing bust 'fore he'd even git in."

Red climbed onto the wing and slipped into the leather seat of the forward cockpit.

"Strap yourself in, Red," said Mr. Tompkins. He showed Red how to fasten the belt. "Now, see this joystick?" It was in the middle of the cockpit, in front of Red.

Red nodded.

"It will move of its own accord because I'll be flying the plane," said Mr. Tompkins. "But you're not to touch it."

"I won't, sir. You can trust me."

Mr. Tompkins patted his shoulder. "I'm sure I can."

Then Mr. Tompkins climbed into the rear cockpit. He gave the signal and Mr. MacMillan propped the aeroplane.

Red looked out at the sea of staring faces, some envious, some disbelieving, some impressed. Mac and Alex stood together at the edge of the crowd, grinning at him. Shona Murray's eyes shone. Alex gave him a thumbs-up sign and Red thought his face would near split as he returned it.

The engine caught. It was deafening when you were sitting right behind it. Then the aeroplane began to move down the field. At the far end, the pilot turned the plane around. It began to head down the length of the field, running faster and faster. It jounced and bounced, the struts between the wings vibrating. Then they were lifting off—up into the air, along with Red's heart, the wind flapping and flustering against Red's face, up into the sky.

Red saw the joystick move by itself, but he didn't touch it.

He stared up at the great blue sky, at the few puffs of cloud above them, then down below. There was the field with people dotted in it, faces turned up . . . the house . . . his house from the air, by golly, the dark roof, the barns, the privy. The trees looked like clumps of ferns.

As they flew farther and farther away, the crowd below disappeared. Red gazed down at the long, narrow strips of Island farms, some of the fields patched green with potatoes or turnips; some grey-green with barley and other grains; still others golden with hay; and some deep-green pastures with dots of livestock, along with stands of dense woods. He looked down at the ribbon-like roads, roofs of farmhouses, livestock like ants, and the red cliffs along the shore, interspersed with strips of sand against the brilliant, dancing sea opening wide, right to the horizon. And there, beyond the expanse of the Strait, he could see a thin line of land that was Nova Scotia.

Red fixed his eyes on the horizon, the edge of the world.

His mouth fell open slightly. As they flew on, the thin line of Nova Scotia thickened into visible land. But the horizon kept moving. When you got close to one edge, there was another edge, and then another and another.

On they flew, out over the glistening blue waters of the Northumberland Strait. As they neared Nova Scotia, Red could see green and golden fields, then some dots that grew into houses.

At last the pilot began to turn the aeroplane around. The wing dipped sharply as the plane circled. The struts hummed and vibrated.

Red didn't feel the least bit of fear. Just joy at the rush of air against his face. Exhilaration at the speed. Jumpin' Jerusalem, they had to be flying near eighty miles an hour.

There was nothing, nothing like it in the whole wide world.

Red wanted to hoot and holler, and at last he did.

He turned around and grinned at Mr. Tompkins, who nodded and grinned back. Red knew Mr. Tompkins understood that it was the most perfect, pure moment of Red's life.

Then they were flying over long, narrow Island farms again, with winding red roads. The aeroplane began to descend. With a jolt of surprise, Red saw a field ahead, with a crowd of dots that turned into people.

It was the MacMillans' field. There was the station, where Sprucecliffe Road crossed Berryfield Road, and the train track snaking off in both directions. And was that Gooley's store? There was the roof of the Munns' farmhouse, and their privy where he'd taken shelter during the storm. And his own house.

How small everything looked.

The pilot circled over the crowd, then came in to land. The ground seemed to rush up to meet Red. Lower and lower, the plane flirted with the ground. It bounced a few times, then at last stayed down, speeding along the field.

"Don't move 'til I tell you," hollered the pilot.

The aeroplane gradually slowed, then turned around in a tight arc and came back towards the crowd. Finally it stopped. When the pilot cut the engine, the silence was almost unnatural. Red couldn't believe he was back on the ground again, with the gravity of the earth holding him down.

But the wind up there seemed to have pushed his lips into a permanent smile. He couldn't stop grinning as he climbed out of the cockpit. With his family, friends and neighbours cheering, he jumped to the ground. Red saw Pa hand Mr. Tompkins the five-dollar bill.

"Anyone else for a ride?" asked the pilot.

"How was it?" asked Mac, coming up to Red. His face was a mixture of excitement and pride, along with amazement.

"Yeah, what was it like?" asked Gooley.

"Just . . . just . . . wonderful," said Red. "Are you going up, Gooley? Why don't you go up?" He knew Gooley's family could afford it.

Gooley looked abashed. "Nah, don't fancy it, meself."

Red couldn't understand it. Why would anyone think flying was dangerous? He hadn't been the least bit scared. He glanced at Ma's proud, beaming face. Thank goodness she wasn't all nervous and fretting like Gooley's Ma.

Alex came over and thumped Red's back.

Red stood straight and tall. For once, of the three of them, he'd been the first. The first to ever go up in an aeroplane.

Shona Murray looked at Red and smiled tentatively.

He grinned back. Seemed like she'd finally noticed him.

The only other person who went up for a ride was Cynthia Johnson. Red watched as she got into the aeroplane, and relived his own moments up in the air, with the pure sky around him.

Even when the pilot returned, then bade them goodbye and flew away, Red still felt as if he were up in the air. He watched the plane become a speck in the sky and disappear. When he finally turned around, he saw Shona, looking shyly at him.

He picked up the courage to walk over. "Hello," he said.

"What was it like?" she asked, her blue eyes shining. "Up there?"

"It was . . . it was . . ." He just couldn't find the right word. " . . . somethin' else."

"It looked sublime," said Shona.

Sublime. Red thought she was right smart to come up with a word like that.

"It was that," he said, the words tripping out. "I could see strips of fields, all patches of colour, like a quilt, and roofs of houses, and all of you, like ants, like dots. And the sea, blue and wide like you wouldn't believe. But best of all was the rush of air. It felt like I could touch the sky. It was . . . sublime." He grinned and grinned, then stood around, not knowing what else to say, until he saw Ma and Pa wave him over to head home.

"Well, see you in school," he said.

"Sure, see you later." She smiled, just at him.

For the rest of the day, Red went about his regular chores with his body on the ground but his mind up in the air, and a few times drifting over to Shona Murray.

At suppertime that evening, when the talk turned to Alex's leaving, Red remembered being up in the plane, and how when you got to the edge of the world another edge seemed to appear, and then another and another.

All of a sudden it hit him—the edge of the world was just a trick of the eye. There wasn't any edge, because the world was all connected.

If you kept going, eventually you'd come back.

You'd always come back to where you started from, because the earth was round! He'd known it before, but now he'd seen it for himself.

Something tight inside of him loosened and eased.

Maybe when Alex left—then Ellen, and even Mac—he'd be able to bear it after all.

Maybe, one day, *he'd* be leaving, too. The idea burst over him with the brightness of an egg yolk.

His hands tingled.

Maybe he'd head out to the edge of the world, and keep going and going all the way around, before coming back home.

ACKNOWLEDGEMENTS

I GRATEFULLY ACKNOWLEDGE THE SUPPORT OF the following:

The Ontario Arts Council for their financial support through the Writers' Reserve fund.

The City of Ottawa for their financial support through their Arts Funding Program.

The Canada Council for the Arts for a travel grant that enabled me to attend the Hawthornden Castle International Writers' Retreat, where I worked on this manuscript.

The Hawthornden Castle International Writers' Retreat for a Residential Fellowship, which allowed me the space and time to work on this manuscript, as well as on other works in progress.

Even as it takes a village to raise a child, it takes an extraordinary group of people to nurture a book from conception to final print. I have been fortunate to have been sustained by such a group.

That Boy Red would not have been possible without John Gilmore, my late father-in-law, whose childhood stories were the impetus and inspiration for this book. A master storyteller, John graciously allowed me to draw from incidents in his life and weave them into fiction. He spent hours answering innumerable questions, both basic and arcane, to help me build an understanding of everyday life in the early 1930s. Although Red and his family are fictional characters, I like to think they reflect the spirit of John's family. I am indebted to John, and not just for his help with this book.

I am indebted as well to the late Martin Gilmore, John's brother, who patiently filled many gaps in my knowledge. Also a gifted storyteller, he read the manuscript and provided invaluable feedback. His enthusiasm, hours of input and good-humoured encouragement are hugely appreciated.

As always, I am grateful to my husband, Ian, for his unfailing love and support. He helped me evolve some of my ideas for this novel, offered sage advice on many a niggling detail and was my first source of reference on Island matters. I am also grateful to Robin, Karen and Ian Paul for cheering me on, and for our joy-filled times together.

Acknowledgements

I owe huge thanks to my brother-in-law Brian Sanderson, for so generously sharing his deep and extensive knowledge about farming. He provided crucial details about crops, farm routines, Island expressions and more. He also read the manuscript for accuracy. His measured responses to my volleys of questions, his keen eye and his fine understanding of nuance were enormously helpful and much appreciated.

I am deeply grateful to the late Janette MacCullough, to Harold MacCullough and to Dianne Baker for sharing their knowledge of Island life, their comments on the work-in-progress and their heartening encouragement. My thanks, also, to Alan Buchanan for his thoughtful exposition on the effects of the Great Depression on the Island. My warmest appreciation, as well, to the many other extended Gilmore family members, too numerous to mention, for their input, interest and support.

I am indebted to the Canada Aviation and Space Museum in Ottawa for information pertaining to the Gipsy Moth. My thanks, in particular, to Ian Leslie, the library assistant at the museum, for filling in specific details about planes of that era and for vetting the relevant parts of this novel.

As well, I am grateful to the Cumberland Heritage Village Museum in Cumberland, Ontario, for their wealth of fascinating material about rural life in the 1930s.

Many other friends and colleagues bolstered me through the writing of this book, and they have my profound gratitude. In particular, I'd like to thank the following:

Karleen Bradford, for her insightful feedback on several drafts of this manuscript, and for her cheerful and reassuring belief in this book.

James Bradford, for sharing his practical aviation knowledge.

Lynne Missen, my wonderful editor, for championing Red and his family, and for her perceptive editing.

Sarah Howden, Catherine Marjoribanks, Noelle Zitzer, Melissa Zilberberg and the entire team at HarperCollins Canada, for their on-going dedication and hard work.

Marie Campbell, for her comments on part of the manuscript, and for being the agent for this book.

And finally—and perhaps in a strangely circuitous manner—I am indebted to L.M. Montgomery, whose stories about Island life were my favourites as a child and, in part, my inspiration for going to Prince Edward Island, where I met my husband . . . and the rest is history. Or another story behind the story.

While I'm indebted to many people for information about P.E.I. life in the 1930s, any errors herein are solely mine.

Several books provided useful information about Island life during the period of this novel, or about the flavour of rural life in general. These works include the following:

Prince Edward Island Sayings, by T.K. Pratt and Scott Burke. Toronto: University of Toronto Press, 1998.

Dictionary of Prince Edward Island English, by T.K. Pratt and Scott Burke. Toronto: University of Toronto Press, 1998.

Leap over Time: History and Recollections of One-Room Schools in the Belfast Area, 1803–1968, by Eliza Gillis, Viola Gillis and Linda Jean Nicholson. Belfast, P.E.I.: Belfast Historical Society, 2002.

Them Times, by David Weale. Charlottetown: Institute of Island Studies, 1992.

Island Sketchbook, by Frank Ledwell. Charlottetown: Acorn Press, 2004.

Echoes of Home: Stories of Bygone Days in Wood Islands, by Ruby MacMillan Matheson, with Marian Bruce. Charlottetown, 2000.

Voice of the Pioneer, vols. One and Two, by Bill McNeil. Toronto: MacMillan of Canada, 1978.

Illustrated Historical Atlas of Prince Edward Island (1880). Belleville, ON: Mika Publishing Company, 1972.